W9-DFG-756

Richard Kennedy:
Collected Stories

Also by Richard Kennedy

AMY'S EYES

THE BOXCAR AT THE CENTER
OF THE UNIVERSE

Richard Kennedy:

Collected Stories

ILLUSTRATIONS BY MARCIA SEWELL

HARPER & ROW, PUBLISHERS

Library of Congress Cataloging-in-Publication Data
Kennedy, Richard, date
  Richard Kennedy: collected stories.

  Summary: A collection of Richard Kennedy's stories,
including "The Porcelain Man," "Come Again in the
Spring," and "Inside My Feet."
    1. Children's stories, American. [1. Short stories]
I. Sewall, Marcia, ill. II. Title.
PZ7.K385Rh 1987   [Fic]   86-45495
ISBN 0-06-023255-2
ISBN 0-06-023256-0 (lib. bdg.)

1 2 3 4 5 6 7 8 9 10
First Edition

for Peter Neumeyer,
a textbook

ACKNOWLEDGMENTS

"The Porcelain Man," text copyright © 1976 by Richard Kennedy, illustration copyright © 1976 by Marcia Sewall. First published by Little, Brown and Company/The Atlantic Monthly Press.

"Come Again in the Spring," text copyright © 1976 by Richard Kennedy, illustration copyright © 1976 by Marcia Sewall. First published by Harper & Row, Publishers.

"The Parrot and the Thief," text copyright © 1974 by Richard Kennedy, illustration copyright © 1974 by Marcia Sewall. First published by Little, Brown and Company/The Atlantic Monthly Press.

"The Wreck of the *Linda Dear*," text copyright © 1979 by Richard Kennedy, originally illustrated by Jim Arnosky, in *Delta Baby & 2 Sea Songs*. First published by Addison-Wesley Publishing Company, Inc.

"The Blue Stone," text copyright © 1976 by Richard Kennedy, illustrations copyright © 1976 by Ronald Himler. Reprinted by permission of the publisher, Holiday House.

"The Leprechaun's Story," by Richard Kennedy, illustrated by Marcia Sewall. Text copyright © 1979 by Richard Kennedy. Illustrations copyright © 1979 by Marcia Sewall. Reprinted by permission of the publisher, E. P. Dutton, a division of New American Library.

"The Contests at Cowlick," text copyright © 1975 by Richard Kennedy, originally illustrated by Marc Simont. First published by Little, Brown and Company/The Atlantic Monthly Press.

"Song of the Horse," by Richard Kennedy, illustrated by Marcia Sewall. Text copyright © 1981 by Richard Kennedy. Illustrations copyright © 1981 by Marcia Sewall. First published by E. P. Dutton.

"The Rise and Fall of Ben Gizzard," text copyright © 1978 by Richard Kennedy, illustration copyright © 1978 by Marcia Sewall. First published by Little, Brown and Company/The Atlantic Monthly Press.

CONTENTS

AUTHOR'S NOTE

"Where do you get your ideas?" That's the question most often asked of writers by nonwriters. My ideas come from memories, images, dreams, stray happenings, but they all have one thing in common: I got the ideas because I was looking for ideas. A person who has it uppermost in his mind that someone is trying to poison him will often enough find that his food tastes a bit peculiar. The anticipation is all. I have included a short note at the beginning of each story to give a notion of how this is.

THE
PORCELAIN
MAN

It was a cold winter. I was living alone in a house that was being torn down. Doors and window frames, stair landings, cabinets, siding, and moldings were lying all about. Plaster littered the floor, and I kept warm by stoking the fireplace with scraps of wood, a sort of cannibalistic rite, the house consuming itself. I wondered about Humpty Dumpty one day. If he had been put back together by all the King's Horses and all the King's Men, could they ever have done it right? And if not—what? Also, after fourteen years of marriage, I was alone, my wife and children elsewhere. Broken up.

ONCE UPON A TIME at the edge of town lived a harsh man with a timid daughter who had grown pale and dreamy from too much obedience. The man kept the girl busy and hardly ever let her go out of doors. "You're lucky to be inside where it's safe and sound," he would say to her. "It's dog-eat-dog out there. The world is full of bottle-snatchers, ragmongers, and ratrobbers. Believe you me!"

The girl believed him.

Each morning the man left the house in his rickety wagon pulled by his rackety horse. All day long he would go up and down the streets of the town, into the countryside and to neighboring villages to find what he could find. He would bring home old broken wheels, tables and chairs with the legs gone from them, pots and pans with holes in them, scraps of this and pieces of that. His daughter would then mend and repair the junk during her long and lonely days inside the house, and the man would take the things away and sell them as secondhand goods. This is the way they lived.

One morning the man left the house and gave his daughter his usual instruction and warning. "If someone passes on the road, stay away from the windows. If someone knocks, don't answer. I could tell you terrible stories." Then he left, and the girl began work on a broken lantern.

Now this morning some good luck happened to the man. As he was passing a rich man's house, a clumsy kitchen maid chased two cats out the front door with a broom and knocked over a large porcelain vase. The vase rolled out the door and down the steps and path, and shattered to pieces against a marble pillar near the roadway. The man stopped, and watched. The maid closed the door. The man waited there for ten minutes. No one came out. Then he leaped down from his cart and gathered up the broken porcelain. He set the pieces gently in his cart and hurried off toward home.

His daughter, as usual, was safe and sound inside. "This is fine porcelain," the man said. "Drop whatever you're doing and patch it up. We'll get a good price for it."

It was early in the day yet, so the man left again to see what else he might find. He remembered to pause at the door and say, "Stay inside. Terrible things are going on out there. Dog-eat-dog, the devil take the hindmost, and so forth." Then he left.

The girl turned a piece of porcelain in her fingers, admiring its beauty. She carefully laid the pieces on a blanket and got out the glue. Then, humming to herself and musing on fanciful thoughts in the way she had acquired from being so much alone, she began to put the pieces of porcelain together. She worked quickly and neatly even though her thoughts were completely elsewhere, and at the end of a couple of hours she was amazed to see that she had just set the last piece in place on a full-sized porcelain man. And at that moment the porcelain man spoke.

"I love you," he said, taking a step toward the girl.

"Gracious!" gasped the girl, snatching up the blanket and throwing it about the man. "Gracious!" she gasped again as the porcelain man encircled her in his arms and kissed her.

While this was happening, the girl's father returned to the house. And right at this moment he opened the door to the room.

"Whoa!" he bellowed.

He grabbed a chair, raised it above his head and brought it down squarely on top of the head of the porcelain man with a blow that shattered him from head to toe, and the porcelain pieces scattered over the floor.

"Godamighty!" the man cried, "I've fractured his skull!" The girl let out a wail, and the man dropped to his knees, stunned with the catastrophe. But the girl explained that it had not been a real man, but only one made of the porcelain.

"A porcelain man who could move!?"

"And he could talk as well," said the girl.

"Fantastic!" said the man. "Quick, put him together again before you forget how you did it. I'll make a cage for him and take him to the county fair. I'll charge a dollar to see him. He can learn to dance. I'll make a big sign saying, 'See the dancing pot,' or something like that. I'll make thousands! Quick, put him together again!"

So the girl collected the pieces on the blanket and slowly began gluing them together again. Her father sat down and watched her for a while, but he found it to be boring and he dropped off to sleep.

The girl worked on, very sad that the porcelain man would be taken away in a cage. She was so distressed by her thoughts that she did not notice until putting the last piece in place that she had built a small porcelain horse. And the horse neighed.

The man woke up.

"What's that?" he said. "That's no man, that's a horse. Now you'll just have to do it all over again. And this time, *concentrate!*" Saying this, the man took up the chair over his head so as to smash the horse.

But the horse said to the girl, "Quickly, jump on my back!" She did, and in a second the horse leaped out the window with the girl, and they galloped across the countryside as the man stood waving the chair at them through the window and shouting words they could not hear.

After running for several miles, the horse stopped in a small meadow, in the center of which stood a tree.

"Get down," said the horse. The girl did. "Now," said the horse, "I will run into the tree and break myself to pieces, and then you are to put me back together as a man again." Then the horse added, "Remember—I love you," and before the girl could say a word, the horse dashed toward the tree and crashed into it at full gallop and broke into hundreds of pieces.

The girl cried out, and then sat down under the tree and wept, for she had no glue.

Now on a path nearby came along a young man pushing a wheelbarrow. He stopped when he saw the girl by the tree, and went to comfort her.

"Don't cry," he said. "Here, let us gather up the pieces and put them in the wheelbarrow. Come along with me and we'll fix everything almost as good as new."

So they loaded up the broken porcelain, and they went to the man's cottage and spread the pieces out on a blanket.

"It must have been a beautiful set of dishes," said the man, and he began to glue some pieces together. They talked as they worked and told each other all about themselves. The girl admired how well and quickly the young man worked with his hands, and in a short while they had put together a dozen dishes, eight saucers and teacups, six bowls, two large serving platters, a milk pitcher and two small vases.

They cooked supper then. Their eyes met often as they moved about. Now and again their hands touched, and they brushed against each other going to and fro.

They set the table with the porcelain ware, and when they were eating, the girl's plate whispered up at her, "I still love you."

"Hush!" she said.

"I beg your pardon?" the young man said.

"Oh, nothing," said the girl.

And they lived happily ever after.

COME AGAIN
IN THE SPRING

One of my favorite movies of all time is Ingmar Bergman's The Seventh Seal, *wherein the good but troubled knight Antonius Block plays a game of chess with Death to keep him off a bit longer, for the knight has something to accomplish, as does Old Hark. Therefore, a game with Death, and a bow to a master storyteller.*

SNOW was on the ground. Old Hark was standing out to the side of his cabin, scattering handfuls of cracked corn and scratch to the birds all around him. Now and then he sniffed the air. It smelled like more snow was coming.

A solitary figure bundled in a great bearskin coat trudged along the forest path to the old man's cabin.

He stopped in front of the cabin and shifted a large ledger out from under his arm. The burly figure opened it to a page, looked at the cabin and then to the page again, and walked out toward the old man.

"Good day," said the stranger.

"Howdy," said Old Hark, brushing his hand on his coat. "Your face is easy, but I can't recollect the name. We met?"

"Not in any formal way," said the stranger. "But I've passed this way before. Maybe you've caught a glimpse of me. I'm Death."

The old man straightened his back and held the feed bag a little closer to his chest.

"Death, eh? Well, you got the wrong place."

"No," Death said, opening the ledger. "You're Old Hark, aren't you?"

"Maybe, and maybe not," said Old Hark, turning his back and scattering a handful of feed.

"Well, certainly you *are*," Death said, taking a pen from his pocket. "It's all right here in the book."

"Don't give a dang what's in the book," said Old Hark. "I ain't going. Come again in the spring."

Death sighed, and took the cap off the pen. "How tiresome," he said. "Everyone tries to put it off, and all it amounts to is making a little check mark after your name." He poised the pen above the book.

Old Hark turned. "I ain't afraid of you."

"No?" Death said, looking up.

"Come again in the spring. I won't hinder you none then. But you see all these birds? Come winter time, they depend on me to feed them. They naturally ought to fly south in the fall but don't, reason that I been feeding 'em all winter since I was no bigger 'an a skip bug. They'd die if I was gone—they ain't real wintering birds. But you come back in the spring, and they'll know I won't be here next winter and have enough sense to go south."

"Oh, that wouldn't do at all," Death said. "The book is all made up in advance. Why, rescheduling you into the springtime would take a good week's work. Erasures would have to be made, new entries, changes of address, causes of departure . . . very complicated, no trifling matter at all, I assure you. No, it really won't do at all."

"Don't know about that," Old Hark said, "but I ain't going." He took a few steps away. Death followed him.

"See here," Death said persuasively, "you're really getting quite old and feeble, you know, quite past the age I usually visit people."

"Ain't going," Old Hark said.

Death saw that the old man was resolute, not at all in the correct state of mind for the business at hand. He considered that he might cause a tree to fall on the old man's head. He consulted his book. Next to Old Hark's name was written: "Means of departure: Quiet, gentle, peaceful." So violence was out of the question.

Death turned a page in the book and studied the entries.

"Now, look," Death said. "I can give you another day. I can fit you in for tomorrow, but then you'll have to come quietly, gently, and peacefully. Even so I'll have to stay up half the night juggling these entries, but I'll do it as a special favor."

"Not tomorrow, either," said Old Hark. "Come again in the spring."

Death was getting impatient. "You're so old now and so feeble and your memory is so shabby you won't even re-member me by then, and we'll have to go through all this again."

"There ain't nothing wrong with my memory."

"Isn't there, now?"

"It's perfect."

Death smiled. "If you think so, let me make you a wager."

"Let's hear it," said Old Hark.

"It's this," said Death. "Just so I can be sure you'll re-member me next spring, let's make a test. If I can ask you a question about something that happened in your life and you can't remember, then you must come with me tomorrow."

"Agreed," said Old Hark. "Ask away."

Death closed the ledger and put his pen away. He smiled again and asked, "On your second birthday, your mother baked up a special treat. What was it?" Then Death turned and walked off toward the forest path. "Good day," he called. "I'll see you tomorrow."

It began to snow. Old Hark returned to his cabin, kicked the snow off his boots and went inside. He put on some coffee to perking and sat back in his rocking chair. He sat there for hours, remembering many things, many smells, and tastes, and sounds, and people, but of course he couldn't remember what his mother baked special on his second birthday.

Some birds chirped outside the door. The snow had stopped. Old Hark got a handful of feed, opened the door and chucked it out. The birds made a fuss of noise, but just as Old Hark closed the door, he heard one chirp above and unlike any of the others, a very strange chirp.

It sounded exactly as if one of the birds had said, "Plum-cakes."

It snowed most of the night. Next morning, Old Hark made his rounds to the bird feeders and scattered plenty of feed. He got his shovel and a ladder out then and climbed up to shove some of the snow off the roof of the cabin.

While he was up there, Death came around with his ledger under his arm. He stood next to the ladder and shouted out a cheery "Good morning!" Old Hark looked down. He put a finger to one of his nostrils, blew his nose in the snow, and then said, "Plumcakes," and turned back to his work.

That was a surprise for Death. He had spent half the night working on the book. He was tired, and now he was angry and was tempted to pull the ladder out from the old man. But he remembered the words in the book, "Quiet, gentle, peaceful," and he got hold of himself.

"Very good," Death said. "I don't think there's one man in a thousand who could have remembered that far back. But of course it might have been luck. Perhaps you just made a guess at it."

"I didn't guess," Old Hark said.

"But you couldn't do it again," Death said.

"I reckon I could."

"Then just to be absolutely positive it wasn't a guess, let's try it one more time."

"One more time," Hark agreed. "Ask away."

"Very well," said Death. "The question is this: On your first birthday, your mother picked some wild flowers and put them in your crib with you. What kind of flowers were they?" And he walked away up the forest path.

After clearing the roof, Old Hark took his shovel to work on some drift that was leaning onto his fence. Now and then he threw some feed out of his pocket to the birds that followed him about. They were singing and chirping around the fence, and as he finished up and headed back to the cabin, Old Hark heard in back of him an unusual chirp, loud and clear.

It sounded exactly as if one of the birds had said, "Buttercups."

Next morning when Death came around, Old Hark was under his lean-to splitting wood.

"Good morning," Death said lightly, although actually he was feeling grouchy because he had been up half the night fixing his book to fit the old man into a new place.

Old Hark spit on his hands and took a fresh grip on his splitting maul. "Buttercups," he said, and swung the maul.

Death swallowed hard to keep from crying out. It was impossible. He would have liked to have Old Hark's wedge jump up and crack his skull, but of course that wasn't in the book. Slowly, Death got control of himself.

"Amazing," Death said. "I can scarcely believe it. What a memory. I'm astounded, really I am. You don't *suppose* you could possibly do that again? I hardly *believe* you could."

Old Hark took a breath and leaned on the butt of his splitting maul. "I reckon I just might," he said. "But supposing I do? Then you got to let me be all the way into next spring."

"Agreed," Death said. "Agreed. Then it's a wager. One more question. If you can answer, then I won't come again until next spring. If you can't answer . . . well, then . . ." Death made a check mark in the air.

"Ask away," said Old Hark.

"The question is this," said Death. "On the day you were born, when the midwife held you up in the air, what were the first words your father said?" Death cocked his head, smiled, and walked away.

After splitting the wood, Old Hark filled all the bird feeders and broke up the ice in the cistern. All the while he was paying close attention to the birds which always fluttered nearby, but he heard nothing out of the ordinary in their chirping. Then he went inside. He stoked up the fire, made coffee, took a nap and puttered with some harness. But every now and then he opened the door and threw out some feed, and listened carefully. Just ordinary singing and chirping. He was feeling especially tired and went to bed early with no answer to the question.

Now the reason the birds could tell him nothing was this. Old Hark had been born in that very cabin, and generations of birds had known him and everything about him, and because of their love for the old man they had passed on many memories of him, and so they knew the answers to the other questions.

But on the day the old man was born, in the very bed in which he now lay, the window was closed and the curtain was drawn, so the birds knew nothing of what his father's first words were upon seeing his newborn son. They could not help him.

Old Hark woke late, which wasn't like him. His bones hurt, and he felt tired. It took him much longer than usual to get his chores done, and the wind seemed to chill him to the heart. Still, he listened carefully to the birds. They said nothing special. Early in the afternoon, without coffee or even a bite to eat, he undressed and got back into bed. He had never felt quite so tired in his life. Through his half-closed eyes, he watched the birds on his windowsill hopping about, but he was too tired even to crack the window a bit so he could hear them sing. Now and then he fell asleep.

Death knocked on the door in the late afternoon.

"Come in," Old Hark whispered.

"Hello?" Death said, opening the door. Then he saw Old Hark laid out in the bed and understood at once that the old man had no answer to the question.

"Well, well," Death said, taking a chair next to the old man's bed and opening his book on his lap. "Now isn't that more like it, yes indeed. Ha, ha. You old rascal, I've been up half the night again on your account, you know, but it's quite all right now, yes indeed. It's good to see you lying there so quiet and gentle and . . ." Death glanced at the book. ". . . so peaceful."

Old Hark paid him no attention. He was watching the birds playing on the windowsill.

"Now," said Death, taking out his pen. "I've managed to fit you in for sunset. Oh, you should appreciate that. It's a choice spot, really. Very appropriate, very . . . *fitting* to the occasion, you know. Daylight ending, the sun going down, darkness coming on. . . . Ah, yes, a choice spot— we usually reserve it for poets." Death ran a finger down the page. "Here we are," he said cheerfully. He took the cap off his pen and moved to make a check mark after Old Hark's name. Then he paused.

"Oh, yes," Death said. "It's a formality, but I must ask you so as to make it all strictly legal. As I recall then, the question was this: On the day you were born, when the midwife held you up in the air, what were the first words your father said?"

But Old Hark had not even been listening. He was look- ing at the birds, and he said to Death, "Open the window."

Death thrust his head forward and clutched at his pen.

"What did you say?"

"Let the birds sing."

"NOOOOOooooooooo!" Death bellowed. He flung his arms about hysterically, splattering ink, then screamed out again and fell off his chair in a fit. He got up in a rage and pitched his book through the window.

Birds flew in, singing. Death grabbed a handful of his coatfront and threw himself out the window and went stumbling up the forest path.

Old Hark leaped out of bed and watched Death disappear into the forest. He was feeling much better. He put on a wool shirt and got some coffee to perking, then cut himself some cheese and bread. In a short time he figured out what all the commotion had been about.

Of course what it was, is this: Death had lost the wager and must leave Old Hark to live until spring, for his father's first words on seeing his newborn son had been "Open the window! Let the birds sing!"

THE PARROT
AND
THE THIEF

This was the first story. I found the basic idea in a book of Laotian folktales, and reset it in New England. I changed several things, including the ending, but essentially, and proper to the mood of the story, it was a theft. "Immature artists imitate; mature artists steal." —Lionel Trilling.

ONCE UPON A TIME in a village by the sea lived a disappointed man who took to stealing things. One day he stole a parrot, which he found in a cage down beside the harbor where the ships sailed in from far lands.

The thief had no use for the bird, but kept it because it was a talking parrot and might tell him of buried treasures or other hidden riches.

He carried the cage home with him, and on that very same day he also stole a sheep from a neighbor and killed it. Part of the sheep he cooked and ate; the rest he hid in his barn.

The neighbor came round that evening seeking his missing sheep, and asked the man if he had seen it. The man replied that he had not, but the parrot spoke up and said, "He killed it, and part of it he hid in the barn," for the parrot was eager to be with his real owner, and off to sea on a ship.

The neighbor found the sheep just as the parrot had said, but the thief insisted, "I did not steal the sheep. The foolish bird speaks lies." And the parrot cried out again, "He killed it, and part of it he hid in the barn!"

Unable to decide between the words of the man and the words of the bird, the neighbor appealed to the law, and a trial was arranged for the next day.

That night, the man put the parrot into a barrel and fastened a cloth tightly across the top. All that night he poured water onto the cloth and beat with a stick on the side of the barrel, which made a deep and rumbling sound. It was a mild night, with the stars and the moon shining brightly, but the parrot in his dark barrel did not know this. When the sun came up the man removed the bird from the barrel and placed it in its cage, and then took it to court as a witness.

When the parrot was called to speak to the court about the sheep, it said as before, "He killed it, and part of it he hid in the barn."

All the people believed the bird.

But the thief said, "Will you put me in jail on the word of a parrot? I know nothing of that sheep. Ask it another question. Ask it what manner of night it was last night."

The question was put to the parrot, and the parrot, remembering the fearful night of the rumbling noise and the drenching water, answered, "Last night came a great rainstorm and much thunder."

Then the people cried, "Certainly the bird cannot be believed!" And the thief was let go with the parrot.

Later in that very day the thief went to another neighbor and stole a chicken, which he cooked and ate, after which he buried the feathers and bones outside the house by the pump.

Searching for her missing chicken, the neighbor came

round and asked the man if he had seen it. "I have not seen your chicken," said the thief, but the parrot spoke up and said, "He killed it and ate it, and buried the bones and feathers by the pump."

The neighbor found the remains of the chicken just as the parrot had said, but the thief insisted, "I did not steal your chicken." And the parrot cried, "He killed it and ate it, and buried the bones and feathers by the pump."

"This foolish bird speaks nothing but lies," the thief scoffed.

The neighbor could not make up her mind who was telling the truth, so she appealed to the court and a trial was set for the next day.

That night, the thief put the parrot into a large tin can and fastened onto it a top with holes in it, and all night long the man packed ice around the can and fanned air over the ice and down through the holes, and the water in the bottom of the can froze. It was a mild night, and the stars and moon shone brightly, but the parrot did not know it. Next morning, the man removed the nearly frozen bird from the can and placed it in its cage, then took it to court as a witness, as he had been instructed.

The parrot was called to testify about the chicken, and it said, the same as before, "He killed it and ate it, and buried the bones and feathers by the pump."

The people were inclined to believe the bird.

But the thief said, "The bird cannot be believed. I know nothing of those bones and feathers. Surely you would not put me in jail on the word of a lying parrot. Ask it another question. Ask it what manner of night it was last night."

The question was asked, and the parrot answered according to its memory of the freezing night, and said, "Last night the cold wind came and water froze to ice."

The people shook their heads and declared, "The words of the bird cannot be believed. The man is innocent." And they let him go with the parrot.

That same day the man stole a pig from yet another neighbor, and killed it and ate part of it, and the rest he hid in his woodshed.

Presently this neighbor came round looking for his pig, and he asked the man if he had seen it about. The man said, "I have not seen it at all," but the parrot spoke up and said, "He killed it, and part of it he hid in the woodshed."

The neighbor found that this was exactly so, but the thief said, "I did not steal the pig. This foolish bird can speak no truth." And the parrot repeated again, "He killed it, and part of it he hid in the woodshed."

The neighbor said that he would let the court decide the matter, and again a trial was set for the following day.

That night, the thief piled some kindling wood around a large cooking pot, into which he planned to put the parrot. He intended to keep a fire burning all night so that the parrot would say to the court next day that the night had been as hot as the hottest day in midsummer. But from the window of the house the parrot saw what the man was about, and understood what had been done to him the last two terrible nights, and why the people of the court did not believe him. After making things ready to fool the parrot again, the man took the bird from its cage and placed it in the cooking pot and closed the lid. He lit the kindling

26

wood then, and after an hour or so of tending the small fire he went to bed, supposing he would let the hot coals do the rest of the work.

The parrot was very uncomfortable inside the pot, but listened closely for the man to leave. Then the parrot managed to pry the lid off the pot and he hopped out. It was a mild night, with the stars and the moon shining brightly.

The bird flew up onto the roof of the house, and for the rest of the night he danced the hornpipe and other sailors' dances he had learned from his real owner, clicking his claws on the roof above the thief's bed. Just before dawn he flew down and climbed into the cooking pot and pulled the lid over his head.

The thief did not wake so early that morning, for with all the noise on his roof he had slept poorly. He replaced the parrot in his cage, then strode off to court once again.

The people now had some reason to doubt the word of the parrot, but they listened as the bird told his story. "He killed the pig, and part of it he hid in the woodshed." The thief was then called to tell his story.

"You cannot put me in jail on the word of this foolish bird," said the thief with confidence. "How should I know how the pig got in the woodshed? Ask it another question. Ask it what manner of night it was last night. If it cannot tell that, it cannot be believed."

The parrot then replied to the question of the court, "It was a mild night, with the stars and the moon shining brightly." Which was true.

The thief was surprised, since he expected that the parrot had spent the entire night nearly roasting in the cooking pot. But he was not worried, and said, "There, you see, the bird is not to be believed. Everyone knows that last night there was a great hailstorm, with the hailstones striking the roof so that a man could hardly sleep."

The court was astonished, and everyone cried out, "Take him away and lock him in jail! His words cannot be believed. Surely he is the thief!"

It followed that the man was locked away for his thieving, and having told his story, the bird was taken down to the dock from where the thief had stolen him. Thereupon his true owner, a sailor who had been grieving for his lost bird, took the parrot up happily onto his shoulder, and they sailed off for far lands on the evening tide.

THE WRECK
OF THE
LINDA DEAR

I was living in a coastal town in Oregon. For a while I worked on a fishing boat, and then was doing odd jobs in the winters. One day I was roofing an old lady's house and had occasion to be in her basement, and in a chalked heart in a small hand was written, "I love you grandpa. Linda dear." So I made up an old man, and occupied my mind with rhyme as I chopped wood, dug ditches, picked moss, and waited for clear skies and calm waters.

Down by the sea where I stroll sometime,
musing on poetry and making up rhyme,
I stopped for a while with a faraway look,
like a poet's picture on the back of his book.

And an old man took me by the sleeve,
and said to me, "Can you conceive
of a rat as large as a sailing ship?"
"No," says I, and he patted his hip
and says, "Sit down and I'll tell you the tale
of the *Linda Dear* and Pacific Bill."

So down I sets myself while he
pulls at his pipe and looks at the sea,
and remembering deeply upon the past,
he stroked his beard and said at last,
"The brass was bright and the paint was new,
and we sailed with a cargo of Mulligan stew."

31

Well, I had better things to do
than listen to lies about a ship filled with stew,
so I said, "Excuse me, please," and got up on a knee,
"but didn't I just hear a bell strike three?"

"Sit down," says he, "and hear me now,
or I'll kick your stern end over your bow!
I've sailed these oceans for forty years,
and I've got some stories not many hears."

So again I sets and he takes my arm,
and begins once more to spin his yarn.

"All rats, you know, are fond of sailing,
they eat the stores and run the railings,
and we fling 'em off when we can, of course,
and watch 'em drown with no remorse.

"But the *Linda Dear*, I tell you, son,
had a thousand rats or it didn't have none,
and they ate up all the Mulligan stew,
and when the last of that was through,
a rat by the name of Pacific Bill
declared he hadn't ate his fill.

"So he ate a friend, and then a cousin,
his grandma next, and half a dozen
other relatives—large and small,
then rats he hardly knew at all,

32

and they sank in his belly in the Mulligan stew,
and his belly grew, and he did, too.

"And thirty rats later old Bill had grown
as big as a hound, and the rats' shrieks and moans
were awful to hear, but they were all through
when they slid down his gullet and splashed in the stew.
Some tried to float on the cabbage leaves,
but they sank, too, in potatoes and peas.

"Then rats came scuttling up the ladders,
and we knocked 'em off as they tried to scatter,
and rats were flying everywhere,
through the rigging and in our hair,
and the mate cried out, 'Look down below!'
and me it was that had to go.

"Oh, never in your life or death
was such a sight to take your breath—
a rat as large as the galley table,
gobbling fast as he was able,
other rats, and he made a catch
to grab my boot, but I slammed the hatch.

" 'A rat, a rat!' to the mate I cries.
'I know they're rats, I've got good eyes!'
'No, no,' I yells, 'this one's a giant!'
'Amusing,' says he, 'but not good science.'
And at that moment the deck busts through,
and Pacific Bill snatched up one of the crew."

The old man then let his head droop down,
remembering this with a tear and a frown.
He looked at me with his eyes all glistening,
"You'll let me know if you're bored with listening?"
"It's fairly interesting," I shrugged and said,
and so he continued, shaking his head.

"Well, Pacific Bill climbed up out of the hold,
and we jumped and ran and climbed and rolled.
He caught the mate and he took a bite,
and I'd never seen that man so excited.
Oh, it's awful to see a rat eat a human,
especially one of your own fellow crewmen.
And Bill chased us all around the ship,
up on the yardarms and out on the sprits.

"One by one he ate up the crew,
and the captain cried, 'Mutiny!' but got ate too,
till I alone, most dead with fear,
was clutching the figurehead of the *Linda Dear*.
I watched Pacific Bill aghast
as he ate the sails, and then a mast.

"He ate the railings, then the deck,
the wheelhouse next and made a wreck
from stem to stern of our good ship,
and my grip on Linda was starting to slip.
Then that monster rat spied me,
and reached out a claw, and I dropped in the sea.

"I fell astern the ship and floated,
watching as that rat grew bloated,
eating everything in sight,
until at last with one great bite,
the ship was gone, and Pacific Bill,
he sank too, and all was still.

"Now I hadn't a raft and I hadn't a dory,
but yet I'm here to tell this story.
Do you want to know," said the man with a wink,
"how I stayed afloat and didn't sink?"
"I wouldn't mind," I said with a yawn.
"If you're in the mood you might go on."

"Well, there I was, doomed to drown,
but just before the third time down,
the figurehead of the *Linda Dear*
popped up beside me, and I'm here
to tell this tale—none truer or straighter,
for hugging that girl till six days later
a sloop named the *Bumblebat* threw us a line,
hauled us aboard, and sailed us home fine."

The old man then lit his pipe with care,
gazed out to sea and said, "It's rare
the way them rats liked Mulligan stew,
and how old Bill just grew and grew,
and I reckon no man living or dead—
but me—ever loved a figurehead.

"So we got married—it was only right,
after hugging Dear Linda six days and nights.
Made a fine wife and mother, in my opinion,
had two lovely girls, and a wooden Indian."

"I'll go now," I said, "if that's the end."
"Aye," says he, "but come back again,
and I'll tell you how ninety-two pigs got free
in a howling typhoon in the China sea."

"Love to hear it," I said, "you bet."
But I've never strolled back that way yet.

THE
BLUE STONE

When I was about seven years old I had a fine and beautiful possession—a blue stone, oval shaped and bright as the sky. For fear of losing it or getting it scratched up, I carried it in my mouth. For one whole day this wonderful, magical thing was mine. I even spoke differently. Then I swallowed it.

Jack and Bertie

"Y̲OU'RE a fool, Jack."

"Could be, Bertie, could be," said Jack. "There's a little truth in most all you say, darling."

Jack was in the stream bed, hitching up his trousers and poking around with his toes, turning rocks over.

"You're a dreamer, Jack."

"You're a beautiful woman, Bertie."

"I'm going back to the house, Jack. I can't stand your foolishment any longer."

"Please yourself, dear."

Bertie kept standing there. "Now what's all these birds fussing about for?"

Jack looked up. "Don't know, Bertie—seems more than ordinary, don't it? Swallows, ain't they?"

A dozen or more small birds were flocking about them and seemed to be concerned with Jack's efforts in the stream.

"You'll catch your death of cold in there splashering about," said Bertie, tucking her shawl a little closer under her arm. "There ain't no signs ever come down from heaven no more, least of all any meant for a ninny like yourself."

Jack straightened up and took a new hitch on his trousers. "Bertie, you should have seen it. It was just about the middle of the night, and I was laying awake looking out the window. And I saw this sparkle in the sky that took off like a shooting star, and it shot across the meadow. Then a little spark jumped off that star and fell down right here over the stream. I think I heard a sizzle when it hit the water. I tell you, it's some sort of a sign."

"Your noggin's loose, Jack," Bertie said. She watched him for a bit longer. "Well, I'll go put some soup on for you, honey. I wouldn't have you dying on my account."

"You ain't bad, Bertie," Jack said, and he watched his wife walk up the path toward the cottage, then continued muddling about in the stream bed.

Bertie hung a pot of soup over the fire and sat down with a piece of mending, and about the time the soup was starting to agitate she heard Jack shout out.

"Bertie, Bertie, I found it!"

He was running up to the cottage in his bare feet. Bertie shook her head and knocked on the side of the pot with the wooden spoon to chase any bad spirits out of it, then turned to watch Jack come slopping in the door.

"Mind, don't come slappering in and break your neck!"

"Look, Bertie," said Jack, pulling up a chair to the table. "It's a real part of a star from heaven, I swear it is!" He opened his hand. There in his palm lay what looked like a blue agate.

"Give it here," Bertie said, holding out the spoon. Jack

put the stone in the spoon, and Bertie held it up close to her eyes. She sniffed, and ladled the stone out in front of her husband again, then turned to take the pot off the fire.

"You're a fool, Jack."

Jack rubbed the stone on his sleeve. He held it up to the window and peered through it. "Straight out of heaven it come, all lit up like the angels had been touching it, and it's got some blue sky in it yet." He put it up to his ear. "And I believe I can hear some harp music in it, and angels singing."

Bertie set the soup out and took a sip of hers, watching her husband.

"Bertie, it's a gift from Saint Peter himself I believe. Maybe a button off his very trousers. And them that finds these blue stones is more fortunate than all the kings in China."

"Let's see it again, Jack."

Jack handed it over, and Bertie popped it in her mouth.

"Bertie!" Jack cried.

"I believe it's a soup stone," Bertie said, "and I'm going to swallow it."

"Bertie, don't you dare!"

Bertie stuck out her tongue with the stone balanced on the end of it, then snatched it back in her mouth. "Hee, hee, hee," she laughed. Jack was wringing his hands. And then, though she didn't mean to do it really, she accidentally swallowed it.

And she turned into a chicken, sitting right there in the chair.

"Oh, Bertie!" Jack cried, and he tried to catch the chicken, but it ran into a corner where he couldn't get to it. "Oh, Bertie, my darling," Jack coaxed, "come out and we'll fix you back to yourself somehow." He made a clucking noise but the chicken wouldn't come out. So he got some grain and laid a path for it to follow along, and moved back so as not to frighten the bird. When the chicken came out eating the trail of grain, Jack made a jump at it, but only frightened it up onto a rafter.

"Bertie, my love, come down and finish your soup."

But it wouldn't, and at last Jack fetched a blanket and tossed it over the chicken and brought the chicken down in a bundle and hugged it and kissed it through the blanket. "Oh, Bertie, don't run away from me, I wouldn't hurt you for anything even if you was turned into a cockroach." He got a piece of string and reached up under the blanket and tied an end around the chicken's leg and let it hop out on the table.

"Bertie, you see what I told you? That stone you swallowed was something out of heaven, and you shouldn't make fun of signs. Now what we're to do, I don't know." The chicken appeared to be paying no attention and began pecking at a crack on the table. "Bertie, does you understand me, darling? Flap your wings, Bertie, if you got any sense."

But the chicken made no recognition, and Jack got up and walked around with his head in his hands. "All I can think of, Bertie, is to take you to the city tomorrow and see if we can't find someone to fix you back to your own self."

He got a box, then filled it with straw and stuck it near

the fire and bedded down the chicken with plenty of feed and water. He wasn't hungry himself and sat at the table deeply worried, watching the chicken.

"Look, Bertie," Jack said. "I'll do your mending for you to entertain you, and I'll sing to you." He picked up the mending and sang to the chicken, which was resting comfortably. All the rest of the day he attended to comforting the chicken and trying to amuse it, and then it was time for bed. He knelt down and kissed the chicken on the head and said good night.

"One night as a chicken can't do much harm, Bertie," he said. "And maybe it has a meaning in it somewhere. If the worse happens, I'll build you the finest roost in the world. I love you, Bertie." Then Jack made off toward bed and presently was standing in the doorway in his underwear looking out toward the dark box. "I'm lonesome for you already, Bertie," he said, and then went to bed.

Of course he could hardly sleep. He dreamed of wild dogs and foxes and things that hurt chickens, and kept waking up to listen to the quiet house. A voice finally woke him when there was light in the sky. It was Bertie calling out, "Jack, you good-for-nothing, don't hog the blankets so!"

Jack leaped out of bed and ran to the kitchen, and there was Bertie lying cuddled up around the box trying to keep warm.

"Bertie! You're yourself!"

"I always thought I was," Bertie mumbled. "Now let loose of the blanket."

Jack got down on the floor and hugged her until she started slapping at his face and saying, "Let me be, let me be, what's got into you anyhow?" And then she came wide awake and sat up and looked around. Jack wrapped her up in a blanket and she remembered slowly and started crying.

"Oh, Jack, it was awful. I was changed into a chicken. I remember you was there, and talking to me, but it was like a spoon clappering inside a bowl, and I couldn't understand anything, and I was afraid of being stewed. And Jack, the racket that goes on in a chicken's head you wouldn't put up with."

"I know, dumpling, I know," Jack said, and he got a fire going and battered up some dough for breakfast cakes. "You must be hungry, darling, seeing as you only had a scatter of grain for supper. There's a bit of milk in the pitcher, looks churny but it's good. Wish we had an egg for you, darling."

And then he just naturally looked over to the box, and there in the straw was an egg.

"Bertie! You laid an egg!"

"No! Did I?"

Jack took the egg to the table. "Sure as anything, Bertie, look!"

"Stars and moons, Jack, I really did!"

"You did a beautiful job, Bertie. I never seen an egg so lovely."

"Aw, you're just saying that, Jack."

"Bertie, I never lie to you—it's just the most perfect egg I've ever seen." He held it up to the light to admire it. "What's this? Why, Bertie, I believe it's got something inside of it."

Then at the same time they looked at each other and said, "The stone!"

"Of course!" said Jack. "That's exactly how you became yourself again, by laying out that blue stone into an egg."

"You know, Jack, I had a feeling inside like I was doing something but couldn't figure out what it was."

"Oh, Bertie, it's wonderful. Now we have an egg for breakfast and the stone back again."

"You don't mean to *eat* the egg, do you? Why, Jack, that would be like eating one of my own children. I couldn't do it, never."

Jack thought on it for a moment. "I suppose you're right, dear. Look—you wouldn't want it to go rotten, either, and we can't throw it away with the stone in it, so I'll boil it. It'll be safekeeping from breaking that way and we'll think what to do about it as time goes by."

"You're not *always* a fool, Jack."

Jack put the egg in the teapot to boil. They ate breakfast then, and Bertie told Jack more of what it was like to be a chicken.

"They's awful clumsy and awkward critters, Jack. Why, it was all I could do to keep my balance. Like walking around on a pair of rickety stilts, it was. And pecking— why, it about jolted my brains loose to do it, but I just had to, you know, since it was my nature. And they can't fly worth beans, if you want to know about that. A person don't know how lucky he is, Jack." Bertie sipped at her tea. "Why, it's a blessing just to have lips."

Jack touched her hand and said, "I'm so happy you're not a chicken no more, Bertie."

"Well, it's a great load off my mind, Jack, and that's true."

When the egg was boiled, Jack cooled it in some water and set it in a little dish on a high shelf. They looked at it in wonder.

"Maybe that's what it was for," Jack said, "just to remind us how lucky we are to be people."

"It's a relief, I can tell you that," said Bertie. "A chicken's got no more sense than a scrap sheet."

That night Jack was at work carving a new latch for the door. There was talk around that a robber was in the neighborhood. Bertie was looking in a little mirror as she brushed her hair.

"Jack," she said, laying her hands in her lap. "I'm getting old and wrinkling all up."

"Bertie, you ain't half old yet, and them wrinkles just helps me feel how pretty you are in the dark."

Bertie smiled and continued to brush her hair. Then she stopped again. "Jack?"

"Aye, turnip?"

"What kind of chicken did I look like?"

Jack looked at her. "Bertie, you was the prettiest looking chicken I ever saw in my life."

"You're just saying that."

"Bertie, I never seen such a fine looking chicken. You made my mouth water."

"Aw, you're a fool, Jack."

"I love you, Bertie," Jack said, and went on to carving some more.

Mockersheep

NEXT DAY, Jack rolled out of bed and pulled on his trousers. Bertie was up, setting on some oat mush for break-fast.

"Bertie," said Jack. "If you went and borrowed a bit of salt pork from sister Minn, we could promise it back when it comes killing time for the pig."

"Oh, Jack, I hates to think about it—it's just my favorite pig of all."

"Time comes for everyone," said Jack.

"Aye," said Bertie. She went to the window and looked at the pig down in its slop pen. She thought a minute. "What do you suppose happens when a pig dies, Jack?"

"It gets et by folks, same as we get et by worms."

"Jack, you needn't remind me! And I don't mean that. I mean what happens to its soul?"

"I dunno, Bertie. It gets et by people's souls, I suppose. Will you go ask sister Minn for some salt pork?"

"Going, Jack," said Bertie, and she put on her shawl and went out and down the path and across the road to sister Minn's place. Jack stirred the oat mush slowly and talked to himself. "Course, then what happens to worms' souls? Suppose we do eat pigs' souls, then do worms eat our souls?" Jack shook his head. "Can't be. That'd make heaven full of worms, then. If it was like that, nobody'd bother going there."

"I ain't bothering," said a voice. Jack turned his head. The door was open, and a dark figure was standing just inside and in the shadows. A hand holding a dagger crossed the opening and caught hold of the door and shut it slowly and quietly.

"Set easy," said the man, and he stepped silently over to Jack and put the point of the dagger at his throat. "I likes people what think about heaven and pray and such," said the man. "Makes it easier to sneak up on 'em." The man glanced out the window and around the hut. He was thick waisted and muscular, with stringy black hair and a corner of his mouth tucked into a permanent smirk. He wore a sleeveless leather jerkin with brass studs on it. "Yer heard about me?" he asked.

"The robber that's been about?" said Jack.

"Yers truly. Mockersheep is the name. Yer know how many bones I broke lately?"

Jack wanted to make the man feel proud and at ease. "Two score?"

Mockersheep laughed. "Come nearly," he said. "Where's yer woman?"

"Gone for a bit," Jack said. "You can take what you want and leave."

Mockersheep went to the window. He stepped quickly to the side of the door and laid back against the wall. Bertie pushed the door open in a minute and walked inside. "I spoke to the pig as I passed, Jack," she said. "I told him he was going to heaven soon, and he appeared comforted."

Mockersheep closed the door behind her. "Yer going too, mum, if yer ain't careful now."

"Land!" Bertie cried.

"This is Mr. Mockersheep," Jack said.

"The robber!"

"Yers truly. Yer heard of me, eh? But yer stupid like all the rest." The robber went to the window and opened it and spit. He stood there holding his dagger toward Bertie and Jack, gazing out over the King's roadway. "Stupid like all the rest, thinking robbing is all I'm about. They think all I love is gold, just like their own miserable selves, and it's cause they's stupid and never thought things out." He turned to face them. "Don't yer know, it ain't gold what makes a man happy."

"I never believed it was," said Bertie.

"Then yer got some brains anyhow," said Mockersheep. He pulled Bertie to the window. "Look down in that bunch of trees. My horse is down in there, a big dapple mare. Yer go get her, put her in the shed. Get!" He pushed Bertie to the door, and she went running out.

"Serve up that mush, man," Mockersheep said to Jack. The robber took up the salt pork Bertie had dropped on the table and chawed on it, then went to slopping up the mush Jack gave him. Presently Bertie came back in. Mockersheep turned with his dagger in hand. "Set," he said. Bertie sat with Jack at the other side of the table.

Mockersheep talked as he ate. "They's all stupid, and that's why they'll never catch me. They's always looking for somebody that robs for gold, just like they'd do themselves if they wasn't mewly dogs. Sure, I take gold when I find it. I ain't ignorant. But that ain't it. Believe me, I seen rich people in my time, seen lords and ladies dressed in silk and jewels, I have, and was they happy? Never that I saw. They's all just as fretful and frightened as beggars, but they don't like to show it. What's that egg?" Mockersheep pointed to the egg in the dish up on the shelf.

"Just an old egg," said Bertie.

"Give it here." He took the egg from Jack. "Hard or raw?"

"Hard," Jack said.

Mockersheep cracked the egg on his forehead and began peeling it.

"Stupid," he said. "And I'd be as stupid as them if I was thinking gold could make a man happy. Naw, gold never does it. It's what's inside a man what makes him happy, something deep inside him he got to satisfy that makes a man happy. D'yer get my meaning?"

"I believe it's so," said Bertie. Jack nodded.

"They can take gold away from yer," Mockersheep continued. "Then yer ain't got anything again and yer miserable. What a man's got to do is build on something nobody can take away from him. Something inside." He thumped his chest. "D'yer get my meaning?"

"Like having children and caring for them," said Bertie.

"Like doing work that satisfies you," said Jack.

"Aye," said Mockersheep. "Only for me it's breaking bones. I'm glad yer understand and won't complain when the time comes. Have yer got a decent club I can use?"

Just then there was the rumble of horses down the road.

Mockersheep stood up, clutching the egg in one hand, his dagger in the other.

"That horse in the shed?"

"Aye," Bertie said.

Mockersheep went to the window. "They's coming up

here!" He looked around, then strode over to a closet and kicked a bucket and mop out of it. "Yer lucky," he said to Jack and Bertie. "Yer got a chance not to get yer bones broke, though it's hard for me to keep a promise like that. Them are King's men coming, but yer don't give me up and I won't break yer bones afterwards. That's all." He shut the closet door on himself just as the horses outside came up.

There came a pounding on the door. "King's men," a voice called out. Jack went and opened the door. A big man with gold stripes on his coat stood there. "King's business. Captain Cupper here." He pushed the door farther open and walked inside past Jack. "You, woman," said the Captain, "a bucket of water for the horses." Bertie went out back to draw a bucket. Captain Cupper looked about and sat down at the table. He had his sword drawn and laid it across his knees.

"There's a man we're after," he said, "and the dog'll be robbing somewhere hereabouts." Jack was sitting with his back to the closet. Mockersheep could be out in a leap and at his throat. "You seen anyone strange about?" the Captain asked.

"No, sir," said Jack. "What's his looks?"

"Folks give it different—'bout your size, I should say. Do you have any fresh meat? King's business. You don't, huh? What's this—egg peelings? Give us some eggs, then, King's business. . . . No? No more eggs, just this slop in the bowl here? Well, I suppose we can wait."

Bertie came back in and sat down.

"Bertie, the King's men want a bit of food."

"Cabbage and potatoes," said Bertie, getting up.

"No fresh meat?"

"No meat, sir."

Bertie got the cabbage and potatoes simmering.

Captain Cupper inspected the edge of his sword. " 'Bout your size," he repeated. "Rides a big dapple mare, that's how you'd know him. Mockersheep he calls himself. Breaks bones, he does, after robbing what he can. Blasted strange! We try to trap him with gold, and he goes and robs somebody for pennies and breaks their bones even when they're obliging. Can't figure him out nohow."

"Is there a reward for him, sir?" Bertie asked.

"For Mockersheep?" said the Captain. "No, mum, no reward for Mockersheep at all. The King don't want him. But there's a reward for his head. Ha, ha, ha, ha!" The Captain laughed at his joke and slapped his knee. "Yes, mum. There's a reward for his head. You know how much? All the gold pieces you can stuff in a goat's bladder, and choose your own goat. That's what. And you know what's more? What's more is that I myself had a dream that I was going to get his head, and how's that? There's others out after Mockersheep, but it was me that had that dream. How do you say on that?"

"Dreams is signs, sometimes," said Jack.

There was a clatter and the closet door squeaked. Captain Cupper gripped his sword on ready as the door slowly began to swing open. A duck waddled out and said "Quack, quack, qu—" just before the Captain shouted "Hi!" and with a swing of his sword lopped its head clean off its body.

"Whoops!" Bertie said.

"Fresh meat," said the Captain, as he jammed the tip of his sword into the body of the duck and lifted it over to Bertie. "King's business. You oughtn't to lie to the King's men, woman."

Bertie held the duck tenderly and laid it on a board and began to pluck it. Jack got up to take a look at it, then he opened the closet all the way. A pile of clothes was on the floor, and the dagger laying there.

Bertie got the duck plucked and cleaned and cooked up with the cabbage and potatoes, and the King's men ate their fill.

"Remember," said Captain Cupper, getting ready to leave. "This fellow rides a big dapple mare, that's how you'd know him—ain't sure what he looks like at all, some says one way, some says another. But his head is worth gold. Thank 'ee, mum, for the meat and such." The Captain touched his forehead with his knuckles in a salute, then he was gone with his men. Bertie and Jack sat down at the table and looked at the duck's head where it lay. The duck's beak gleamed like gold where it caught the sun.

The Moon

THE KING'S MEN had been gone an hour. Bertie had dug the blue stone out of the duck's guts and it was laying on the table next to the duck's head.

"Do you honest mean to do it, Jack?"

"Why, certain, Bertie. It's a gift from heaven for us, the

blue stone is. It's all because of it we got this duck's head, worth a goat's bladder full of gold coins."

"It don't look like much, Jack. Do you think the King'll give you all that gold for an old duck's head?"

"It ain't just a duck's head, Bertie—it's that robber's head, Mockersheep's, and that's how it's worth something. And even if it don't look much like him, we got his horse for proof, and the blue stone to prove it out finally, if it comes to that."

"How would that be, Jack?"

"Why, all they got to do is feed the stone to somebody, then they'd see it was the truth how it changes a person."

Bertie set her chin on her hand. "I don't know, Jack."

"You'll see, Bertie." Jack got out a little leather bag and stuffed the duck's head in it, then dropped the blue stone in after it. He got up. "Bertie, I'll be back in a fine wagon, just you wait."

They went out back and led Mockersheep's big mare from the shed, and Jack took the reins. He kissed Bertie. "Now don't worry and don't mope around concerning about me. Go visit sister Minn and tell her we'll give her back a whole pig for that hunk of salt pork." He paused and looked at their goat.

"What are you thinking, Jack?"

"I was figuring, Bertie, if I ought to take a goat's bladder with me."

"No, Jack, I wouldn't let you do it."

"Aye. She's scrawny anyhow. I'll choose one of the King's goats."

He kissed Bertie again and headed off on the King's roadway toward the city. Bertie watched him go up and over a far hill, wiping her hands in her apron with worry. Then she headed down toward sister Minn's place to tell her the whole story and try to act like she thought everything was fine. She didn't, though.

But Jack was feeling good. He was gone a mile or so when he stopped to get a drink from the stream alongside the road. He sat there a minute on his hands and knees looking in the water and dreaming about how rich Bertie and him were going to be. Then it was like a tree had fallen on him. He was flattened out and his head was thrust into the mud. Weights were on his arms and legs, and then one arm was turned up hard against his back, and there was snarling and cussing in his ears.

"Now, you scroggy scrubber, now you'll pay!"

"Tie the blugger up, get him on his feet!"

"Get his bloody dagger away from him, hold his bloody arms!"

Jack was jerked to his feet. Mud was in his eyes, but he could squint and see he had been jumped by some of the King's men, four of them, different ones than had come to the cottage. They whipped his arms around in front of him and tied his wrists with thongs, all the while jolting him in the head and taking turns kicking his legs and knocking him about.

"Bring him up here," a Captain yelled from the roadway, and Jack was led up out of the stream bed.

"Hah!" said the Captain. "We got ya finally, didn't we, ya skuggy dog!"

Jack knew what it was. Because of the big dapple mare, they thought that he was Mockersheep.

"I ain't him!" Jack cried.

"Ain't who?" said the Captain.

"Mockersheep, I ain't him!"

"Yah, in a pig's satchel ya ain't." The Captain got down off his horse and drew his sword. "Fetch him over to yonder stump, men."

They drug Jack over to a tree stump and forced him down on his knees next to it. One of the men grabbed his hair from the other side of the stump and plunked his head on its sideways. Another ripped his shirt and laid bare his neck.

"I was going to see the King," Jack pleaded. "I was taking him Mockersheep's head."

"Yar, well never mind that, we'll take it for ya and say ya sent it. It'll save ya the trip."

Jack knew he didn't have a chance to explain. The Captain planted his feet apart and took the sword in both hands.

"Last words!" Jack cried. "Last words!"

"Yar, I suppose," said the Captain. "Say and be done with it."

"A man ought to get a last meal. You know that's so. And all I want's a bite, just a taste before you cuts my head off."

"We ain't sparing no food for the likes of ya," the Captain said.

"Let my head up a little. I got a bite to eat here with me. Bad luck if you don't."

"Aw, let him up a little," said the Captain. The men

loosened their hold and Jack took the little leather bag from his belt.

The Captain eyed him suspiciously. "Careful, now," he said.

Jack dug in the bag and took out the duck's head.

"Ugh! I knew ya was a rotten dog, but eating a *duck's* head. Ugh!"

Jack laid the head on the stump and dug to the bottom of the bag and got his fingers on the blue stone. Then before they could see a thing he dashed it up and into his mouth and swallowed it.

And he was a duck.

His clothes fell from him and he sprang off flapping and quacking between some legs and down the bank to the stream. He fled over the water, running and swimming and flying, and off across a field and into some woods. This while, the King's men stood around yelling and cussing at each other about what happened and claiming the others had gone crazy because each thought he'd gone crazy himself, seeing a man turn into a duck. And only after a bit did they come to agree it had happened and was magic, and decided to give chase, but by then the duck was out of sight and lost to them.

Jack, the duck, hid in the woods till it started getting dark, and tried to collect his thoughts, but could only think in quacks and couldn't understand the language. Except he did know he had to wait till dark and then get home. The moon was starting to come up when he left the woods.

He ran on back to the stream, then up and across the

King's roadway after looking carefully both ways for any King's men who might be out. He ran hard for a while, then, and almost stumbled onto a couple of men sitting on a cart at the side of the road smoking their pipes. They were talking. Jack hid in some brush.

"They's gone mad, I tell you!"

"It's the moon," said the second man, indicating the full moon with the stem of his pipe.

"I don't know about that, but they's gone mad. They come riding up and without no word they chased down six of my ducks and chopped their heads off. Then they just stood there looking at the carcasses for a while and rode off. They did the same over at Amos's place and all up and down the road I hear."

"They don't say nothing?"

"Well, they's cussing all the time, of course, being King's men, and calling the poor ducks dirty dogs and scurvy robbers and suchlike. They's mad, I tell you."

"Probably," said the second man. "I figure it's the moon."

"Either that or the end of the world."

"One or the other," said the second, sucking on his pipe.

Jack cut around the men and ran on and got to the cottage door in another ten minutes. He clobbered at the door with his head and beat his wings on it. Bertie opened it.

"Now what's all this?"

Jack ran inside under her legs and jumped from table to chair, generally banging himself around the place, upsetting bowls and boxes and making a terrific amount of quacking and squalling. Bertie took up a broom and started swinging at him and knocked things about this way and that. She tired before she could bash him and sat down for a minute to rest. Jack gave up flapping and crashing about, which wasn't proving anything and was likely to get him brained. Then he did the right thing. He went to the closet and sat down in amongst Mockersheep's clothing and just sat there looking at Bertie pitifully, nudging his beak into a shirt sleeve and looking at Bertie to understand.

She was still catching her breath. "I'll slam you good next time, just you wait," she said, and she got up slow and meaningful and edged up on the duck with the broom ready. Then she caught on.

"Jack!" she cried, dropping the broom. "Is it yourself? Oh, Jack, you et the stone, didn't you? Jack, why'd you do it?" She picked the duck up and set it on the table to study the problem. "You can't lay an egg, Jack, you know you can't do that. It wouldn't be proper and gentlemanly." She thought for a while. "You'll have to trust me, Jack. Try to remember you're just a dumb beast and I know what's best, no matter what happens."

She got some twine and tied it around the duck's feet. She laid it on its side while she made a good knot and let out another long end of twine. She hummed to the duck to keep it calm. Then she hung the duck upside down from a rafter and wrung its neck while she beat it with a stick, and out plopped the blue stone onto the floor, and in a second afterwards Jack came pitching down after it, naked as a snake, and knocked himself out completely.

Bertie put a wet rag on his head and covered him with a quilt. The blue stone she set on the table and for a long while sat watching Jack. Then she went to bed.

Adrian

JACK lay in bed all the next day and Bertie cared for him. She sat and held his hand and listened to his story.

"And Bertie, I'm just so sore all over from being kicked and knocked about and having my neck stretched out by them and then wrung by you and beat by yourself, too, and falling on my head—I honest think we ought to throw that blue stone back in the stream where I found it and let heaven help someone else out for a while. I'm tired of it."

"It's been a misery for you, Jack darling, but that's because we didn't know what that stone was for. It's got miracles in it, sure, and all we got to do is find out how to use it. Now when I told sister Minn how it changed people into ducks and chickens and such, she pulled at that long hair on her nose and seemed to remember something, and what she remembered is that she heard one of those singing men, those minstrels, singing out a song about such a stone, right there in the city not only last week."

Jack came up on an elbow. "Well, then, what did he sing?"

"Sister Minn says she can't remember. She said it was a song about ducks and chickens and things falling out of heaven, all about the blue stone and how it's supposed to be if you find one."

"Just so?"

"Near as she remembered. She tried to get the words of the song up but couldn't—pulled that nose hair right out thinking on it."

So Jack and Bertie decided he'd have to go to the city and hunt up the minstrel and hear the song about the blue stone. He lay in bed for a day more before his bones felt well enough to make the walk. Bertie packed some dinner for him, and he tied up a blanket to sling over his shoulder in case he should have to spend a night on the road, or in the city. Then he took their savings, just a few coppers, and made to leave. Bertie straightened his collar and patted his buttons.

"Be careful, Jack, and you're sure the King's men won't know you?"

"I had mud all over my face, Bertie."

"Now mind, if you see the King and Queen, fill up your eyes with it. I want to know just everything about how they look, and what the Queen was wearing, and does she have tiny feet, and all you can remember, Jack."

"Aye, Bertie." He stood ready to go. Bertie looked him over once more and then kissed him, and he was off. They waved at each other when Jack turned off onto the King's roadway. Bertie started humming to herself and fixing things up around the house.

Jack passed and greeted people on the road but saw no King's men. It was late afternoon when he arrived in the city. He walked up and down several winding streets asking where he might find the minstrel man, and at last found a dusty boy in a rag of a jacket who could tell him. First, the boy looked him up and down very careful. He had a wily way about him.

"For a penny, sir, I'll tell you where to find him."

Jack tossed him a penny.

"Over in yonder inn, in the alehouse most like. Another penny, and I'll sing you a song myself."

"Do you know one about a blue stone?"

"I know one about a blue dog."

"Thank you all the same," said Jack and headed for the inn, which was called the Silver Plate. He went into the alehouse.

Jack stood for a minute till his eyes got used to the darkness inside, and then he saw his man without asking for him. He was thin, with long sandy hair parted in the middle and a moustache that hung down on the ends nearly to his chin. A lute was sitting on the table, and he was taking a gulp off a large tankard when Jack walked up to him. The man wiped his mouth with the back of his hand and cocked an eyebrow at Jack.

"Are you friendly to the people's cause, sir?" he said.

"I . . . I think I am," said Jack, not knowing what the man meant, but he liked people and supposed it was something about that.

"Sit, then. And if you wasn't, we could toast the King. But let's do that anyway. Innkeeper!" The innkeeper, a bald and bulgy man in an apron, came over with two tankards of ale. The minstrel waited for Jack to pay for them, then he lifted his tankard. Jack did so, too. "A toast to the King," said the minstrel, "that he may be toasted better later on." He winked at Jack and took a deep draught of his ale. Jack drank too.

"Do you know the King?" asked Jack, mindful of the news Bertie wanted.

"Aye, I know him," said the man. He licked his forefinger and snapped some spit on the floor.

"What's he like, then?"

"An oaf, sir, an oaf. You have the word of one who knows grace."

"And the Queen?"

"Ugly. You have the word of a man who loves beauty. But you didn't come up so directly for that news. What's your business?"

"My name is Jack, and my wife Bertie and me . . ."

The man put out his hand. His sleeve was patched with different colored cloths. "Adrian is my name, sir, as honest a man as they come nowadays, and that is no compliment to myself."

"I come for a song," Jack said, "a song about a blue stone."

"Ah, yes," said Adrian, "a blue stone." He took another long drink, then reached for his lute. He looked out the window for a bit, moving his lips quietly. "Hmmmmmmmm. How about if it's a blue rock, Jack? I can get more rhymes out of rock than stone."

"But I didn't want you to make up a song," Jack said. "I thought you knew a song about a blue stone, and that's what I was after."

"No. No, I don't. But I'd be pleased to learn it, Jack. How does it go?"

"Ah, I don't know either," said Jack, putting his head in his hands. "An old lady said she heard you singing a song about a blue stone, with ducks and chickens in it also."

"I'm sorry, Jack," said Adrian, "but I don't know such a song." He took a gulp of his ale. "But here's one about a blue dog you might like," and he strummed his lute.

"No, not that," said Jack. "Are there others in the city like yourself?"

"Minstrels? No, I'm the only one right now. It's a poor city."

Jack finished up his ale. "It's been nice, anyway," he said.

"My pleasure, sir," said Adrian and began strumming softly on his lute as Jack walked away. He was almost to the door when Adrian called out, "Wait a minute. Come back!" Jack returned to the table. "Did you say this song had chickens and ducks in it?"

"Aye, it should."

"Well, I do know a song with chickens and ducks in it. Not so much a real song—more like a riddle, I've always thought. But it goes like this." Adrian stroked a chord and sang, " 'When heaven is falling, the pieces are blue . . .' "

"That's it, that's it!" Jack cried.

"What? How can you know that? I haven't even come to the chickens and ducks yet."

"Go on, go on," Jack said.

Adrian began again:

> "When heaven is falling, the pieces are blue,
> and under your tongue, a poem will come true,
> if man be the first to find it but heed,
> nor use it in vengeance, nor anger, nor greed.

"But heaven is not for the swallows of men,
a duck for a man, for a woman a hen,
but swallows for swallows and wings for the new,
born of the angels, the pieces are blue."

Jack sat so earnestly silent at hearing it that Adrian didn't say anything, just continued strumming quietly and looking out the window.

"It's hard to understand," said Jack.

"Aye," Adrian said. "It's an ancient song. A very old man taught it to me, and he himself was taught by an old man."

"But what does it mean?" asked Jack.

"I don't know and the old man didn't know. But somebody will, somehow, somewhere, so I sing it now and again. It's like carrying a message around with you, with no address you see, but it'll find its way to who it should." Adrian looked at Jack with great curiosity then. "Do you know what it means?"

Jack rubbed his chin. "Parts of it. I can tell you that the pieces of heaven are blue stones, I know that. And then that part about swallows and men . . ."

" 'But heaven is not for the swallows of men'?"

"That's it. Those aren't birdlike swallows, but that means that you shouldn't swallow one of these stones."

"Oh? And why's that?"

"Because if you do swallow one of these stones, you turn into a duck, and a woman turns into a hen."

"Ahhhhhh," said Adrian.

"But the rest of it I don't know," said Jack. "Could you learn it to me?"

"Certainly," Adrian said. He beckoned to the innkeeper and recited to Jack. "We'll take it two lines at a time. First this: 'When heaven is falling, the pieces are blue, and under your tongue, a poem will come true.' "

Jack repeated the lines, and they sat there drinking and saying the song back and forth for a time. It was dark out now, and Adrian closed the shutter on the window. The innkeeper came over once and touched Adrian on the shoulder. Adrian looked up and nodded and continued teaching Jack the song.

Then the door burst open, and the same young boy who had told Jack where to find Adrian jumped inside and yelled out "Zork's man, Zork's man!" and jumped out again.

Adrian took a last quick gulp of his drink and flung open the shutter and window. He grabbed his lute by the neck and hopped nimbly up on the table and put a leg out the window. He turned and said to Jack, "Have you got it now?"

Jack nodded. "But what's happening?"

Adrian winked and dropped lightly to the ground. The innkeeper took the empty tankard and made a quick wipe of the table where Adrian had been sitting. Hardly had he finished this when a large dark figure thumped through the door. The three or four other men in the place hunched themselves around their tankards and tried to seem like they weren't paying anything any mind, but the place was heavy with nervousness. It was Zork's man. He had a broad face and his eyes glinted deep in their sockets like rats running around in a dungeon. The glints fell on Jack. The man walked over and put his knuckles against Jack's head and turned his face to get a look at him.

The innkeeper came over. "He's just a country man, come in for drinking is all."

The large man snorted like he didn't believe it, and looked at the open window. He wiped a finger on the table where Adrian had been sitting, and put the back of his hand to the bench to feel if it was warm. Then he looked carefully at Jack again and went around behind him. He circled his great hands lightly around Jack's throat and said, "Whoever next sees that songbird, tell him I want him to sing the frog's song for me. It goes like this—CROAK! CROAK! CROAK!" At each "croak" the man tightened his stranglehold, and when he let go, Jack gasped and slumped on his bench. The man turned and went out without another word.

The innkeeper sat down. "Are you all right?"

"Aye," said Jack, "but my neck's getting some hard wear these days. Who was that?"

"Zork's man. Zork's the King's magician or sorcerer or whatever you might call it. But call it what you will, he's no good anyway, losing his powers and getting into blackmail, and making honest folk pay protection money and such. And worse. A bad fellow. Now he's after Adrian because of some little songs Adrian has been making up and passing around. Adrian makes people laugh at Zork, and Zork wants to kill him."

He closed the window and looked toward the door. "You'd better go, but I wouldn't stay in the city if I was you. Walk wide around corners and get out on the roadway and you'll be all right. I believe he thought you were a friend of Adrian."

Jack took up his blanket roll. The innkeeper went out the door and whispered loudly, "Pin! Pin!" He came back to Jack. "Follow the lad. He knows the best way to the gates." He put his hand on Jack's shoulder. "Godspeed, friend."

When Jack came out the boy turned and skipped up the street. Jack had to trot to keep up with him. Dark and careful cats crouched in wonder to see people moving along the night streets as quickly and slyly as themselves.

Poetry

THE BOY left Jack at the city gate, and Jack walked the King's roadway for an hour before he dared to bed down. He slept cold, then very early took to the road again. Over and over he recited the song about the blue stone, and his excitement grew as he believed he had solved most of the riddle.

The sun was only a cock crow high when Jack arrived home. He entered quietly, but Bertie awoke when he neared the bed.

"Shhhh," said Jack, putting a finger to her lips. "I've got to sleep, love, but I've learned the song about the blue stone. Sister Minn was right—there was a minstrel named

Adrian, and Zork's man was after him . . . and other things. But I've got to sleep now, love."

Bertie was impatient to know everything, but she let Jack sleep two hours before holding a cup of hot broth under his nose. Jack sipped the broth and munched a crust of bread while he told Bertie the story.

"Oh, Jack, you're lucky to be alive."

Jack piled out of bed and pulled on his clothes. "Where's the stone, Bertie?"

Bertie got the stone and Jack studied it at the table with even greater interest than ever.

"Now, do you understand the words of the song, Bertie?"

Bertie folded her hands in front of her like a schoolgirl. "Tell me again, Jack."

"Well, some of it's plain enough. The first line says, 'When heaven is falling, the pieces are blue.' Of course the stone is one of those pieces." Bertie nodded. "Then the part of it that says, 'But heaven is not for the swallows of men, a duck for a man, for a woman a hen'—that part we know from what's already happened. It just means that nobody ought to swallow one of these pieces of heaven— one of these blue stones—because of changing into a duck or a chicken."

"That's the truth, Jack."

"But now listen, Bertie," said Jack, laying his hands flat on either side of the stone. "Here's the first part complete:

"When heaven is falling, the pieces are blue,
and under your tongue, a poem will come true,

> *if man be the first to find it but heed,*
> *nor use it in vengeance, nor anger, nor greed.*

There, do you see it, Bertie?"

Bertie frowned. "Not all, Jack, but it sounds like a warn-ing. Maybe we shouldn't have tried to get that gold off the stone's working, since it was from heaven and all."

"Right, Bertie, I believe it's so, since you might call that greed. But still it's wonderful, Bertie. It sounds to me like the song says that if you put the stone in your mouth—under your tongue—then whatever poem you say will come true! Open your mouth, Bertie."

Bertie did, and Jack dropped the stone in.

"Careful and don't swallow it. Put it under your tongue. Can you talk, darling?"

"Aye, it lays there nice."

"Now, Bertie, you're to say a poem, and we'll see if it comes true."

"A lullaby, Jack?"

"No, Bertie, that wouldn't do it. It might just make us fall asleep and there's not much to that. Make up a poem, Bertie."

"Ah, Jack, I can't hardly do that."

"Sure you can, Bertie. Just try and think of something now and I will, too."

Jack got up and walked around the table several times with his arms behind his back. Bertie sat with her eyes shut squinty-tight and her hands clasped in her lap, thinking. "Quork! Quork!" Their pig nosed open the door and Jack was about to shoo it out when he thought better and said,

"Soooooo, pig, sooooooo," sweetly, and the pig came in.

"Bertie, make up a poem on the pig. There's lots of words that go with pig—big, dig, fig, sprig, swig. . . ."

Bertie opened her eyes and concentrated on the pig. Jack got it a cob to make it stand still.

"I don't get nothing, Jack," Bertie said, breaking off a crust of bread from the loaf on the table. She put it on the floor for the pig. "Jack . . . ?"

"Aye?"

"What was it Adrian said about the King?"

"He didn't like the King, Bertie. He didn't say much."

"What did he call him, though?"

"An oaf, dear, and called the Queen ugly."

"Hmmmmmmm," said Bertie. "Can the poem be silly, Jack?"

"Aye. It's only to see if we're right about how the stone works."

Bertie nodded her head up and down several times like she was keeping time, then she said, "I've got it, Jack." And she said a silly poem:

> "The Queen is ugly,
> and the King is an oaf,
> and this poem might change
> a pig to a loaf."

And right in front of their eyes the pig disappeared as fast as a balloon popping, and where it had been was a large loaf of bread.

"It worked, Bertie! It worked!" Jack hugged Bertie and

inspected the loaf, and it was real bread. After their excitement died down, they agreed that even if it was magic, it was all in all something of a loss. The pig was worth more than the loaf. However, they decided that if one poem could change a pig to a loaf, another might change it back again, and to this end Bertie and Jack worked at making up a new poem, and at last they had it. Bertie, with the blue stone under her tongue, said the poem at the loaf of bread.

> *"The King is wise,*
> *and the Queen is pretty,*
> *and this poem might change*
> *a loaf to a piggy."*

And they had their pig back again.

"Darling!" said Bertie and kissed it, then poked it out the door and got some flour and a couple of pans out of the cupboard. She was going to bake some bread.

It was true. The blue stone had the magic in it to change anything in the world to anything else if only you could make up a poem to say how you wanted it to be.

> *. . . but heed,*
> *nor use it in vengeance, nor anger, nor greed.*

Pigs

IT WAS early in the day yet when Bertie called Jack in from the garden. She had two fresh loaves of bread cooling in the window.

"Is it greed, Jack, for us to give a pig to sister Minn?"

"Why no, Bertie, that's a gift. That's a nice thing to do."

"And how about if we make a pig for ourselves, Jack?"

Jack pulled on his ear and thought. "Just one, Bertie? No, I think that would be all right. Greed means wanting to get a whole lot of things for yourself, more than you need. It'd ease life a little having another pig. I don't think you could call that greed."

"Good!" Bertie set the two loaves on the floor and said the correct poem first at one loaf, then the other, and they had two fine plump pigs. "Do you suppose, Jack, if I'd put cloves in the bread, the pigs would already be seasoned?"

Jack had no idea on that and went out to work in the garden. He was puzzling on the song of the blue stone— the two last lines that he hadn't figured out:

> but swallows for swallows and wings for the new,
> born of the angels, the pieces are blue.

Over and over he said the words to himself, and would stop and lean on his hoe and look off in the distance for a while, then shake his head and go back to work.

Bertie tied a blue ribbon on the tail of sister Minn's pig and put a rope around its neck. She hefted the other pig up against her side and led off on down the path. After she dropped their own pig into the slop pen, she crossed the roadway and headed over to sister Minn's with her gift pig.

Sister Minn was angry. She was delighted with the gift pig but got to grumbling again soon about one of her neighbors, an old lady who lived on the other side of the fence, called the Old Magger. She was a strange and scratchy old lady who always wore a hood to stay out of the light. Some said she lived on toadstools and nothing else, and she was always rummaging in the woods, picking at the ground and at the trees, collecting bones of little animals, tearing bird nests apart for a few twigs she wanted, trapping squirrels and cutting off their tails, and digging up roots. Some nights she sat and carried on hooting conversations with owls. She lived in a dirty shack and had a few pigs which she let run and root where they could. One of them had got through the fence and rooted up sister Minn's garden. That's why sister Minn was angry. But it didn't do to argue with the Old Magger. She was full of threats and would cook up some sort of potion to use against anyone who crossed her. She knew some dark things, and people were afraid of her, but folks now and then in desperation would go to her for help. For the payment of a basket of vegetables, they might come away with a small bottle of green liquid or a twisted root that would change somebody's mind or health.

And so because sister Minn was angry at the Old Magger, Bertie was too, and now she had a little bit of magic herself. Therefore, when she left sister Minn's, she walked along the fence until she came upon one of the Old Magger's

74

pigs, and she changed it into a loaf of bread. "That'll teach her," Bertie said and chuckled.

She was walking along the roadpath when along came a farmer from the opposite direction. He was carrying a suckling pig wrapped in a blanket, taking it to sell in the city marketplace. It was narrow there, and he bumped Bertie off the path into the ditch and hadn't time to beg her pardon. Bertie was about to cuss him but then changed her mind.

"Good farmer," Bertie said from the ditch. "Sir, is that a suckling pig you have there?"

"Aye," said the man. He stopped, hoping to save himself a journey to the city. "Do you want to buy a pig?"

Bertie pulled herself out of the ditch and approached the man.

"Is his nose pink? Is his eyes clear?" she asked.

"Look for yourself," said the man.

Bertie took the blue stone from her apron pocket and put it under her tongue. Then she lifted a fold of the blanket and looked in on the pig. She put her head down near to it and whispered. She folded the blanket back in place.

"No thank you, I think not," she said. "He looks a bit rude."

"Bah!" said the man and strode off.

Bertie was laughing when she arrived back at the house. Jack was separating some seeds at the table. "What's funny, Bertie?"

She told him about changing one of the Old Magger's pigs into a loaf of bread and was going to tell him about changing the farmer's pig, too. But Jack didn't think the story about the Old Magger's pig was funny at all.

"Bertie, you shouldn't have done it."

"Aw, Jack, she's got plenty of pigs—and I was just getting back for how sister Minn's garden got rooted up."

"That's just it, Bertie. That's vengeance—getting back at someone is. Now that's a warning in the song, Bertie, and we've had enough trouble already from not being careful with the stone."

"Aw, Jack, it was only an old pig, and she deserved it."

"Bertie, even if it wasn't a warning in the song, I wouldn't mess around with the Old Magger. She's strange, Bertie. You never know what sort of bad luck she may lay on a person. Give me the stone, now, and I'll go back and change that loaf back into a pig."

"I'll *do* it, Jack, if you're going to worry and make such a fuss. But in my mind, it wouldn't hurt for somebody to change the Old Magger into a pig, if you want to know how I feel."

"Just change that loaf back, Bertie. I think it's best. It appears there's more mystery about that blue stone than we know even yet, and we ought to be real careful."

So Bertie left, and Jack set picking over the seeds and saying the song of the blue stone to himself. Presently Bertie returned.

"Did you do it, Bertie?"

"Almost, Jack. The field mice had been at the loaf, but they skitted off. Hadn't ate but just a corner off, so I said the poem and it changed into a pig all right, but he only had three legs. He got along tolerable, though, and went stumbling on back where he came from. Do you suppose that's fair enough, Jack?"

"Well, we put it right the best we could, Bertie."

Bertie started working on the seeds with Jack, and she thought about the farmer carrying his loaf of bread to the city market, and she giggled.

"What's funny, Bertie?"

"Oh, this and that, Jack." No, she wouldn't tell him about that. There was no way to correct it, and of course she had been angry when she did it, and that was warned against in the song.

Now the farmer himself hadn't noticed anything and continued on his way. He arrived in the marketplace and sold his pig at the regular place. But as he was walking away with his money, the shopkeeper uncovered the bundle and found only a loaf of bread.

"Hey! You rogue, come back here! Do you mean to sell me a loaf of bread for a pig?" He grabbed the farmer by the neck and got a stick to beat him. The man swore that it *had* been a pig, but that it had been bewitched by a woman along the King's roadway. The shopkeeper shook the money out of the farmer and beat him soundly, and gave him a little extra for telling such an outrageous story.

No one paid it much attention. It seemed that someone was always beating someone else with a stick, and the farmer crawled into a doorway to nurse his bumps and bruises. Yet one person had noticed the whole affair. Zork, the magician to the King, had been lurking about in common clothes, eager to learn some of the subtle magic that goes on in marketplaces. This appeared to be very interesting business to him. He picked up the loaf where it had fallen aside in the scuffle and slid down next to the farmer.

"Friend," said Zork. "Is it true that a woman changed your pig into this loaf of bread?"

"True enough to get me a beating," said the man, rubbing spit onto a scraped knee.

"Could you tell me where I might find this woman?"

"I could. For the price of a pig."

"Done," said Zork and paid the man. The farmer then explained to the magician exactly where the pig had been turned into a loaf and what Bertie looked like and how they were right near the cottage path. Zork took the loaf to his quarters and called for his man.

Jack was waiting to fall asleep, hoping he might have a dream that would unpuzzle the rest of the song about the blue stone. The last lines kept running through his head:

> but swallows for swallows and wings for the new,
> born of the angels, the pieces are blue.

Bertie giggled, thinking of the farmer.

"What *is* funny, Bertie?"

"This and that, Jack, this and that."

But she would not have thought anything was so funny if she could have seen the man standing in a grove of trees nearby looking at the dark cottage, his rat eyes glinting.

Zork

NEXT MORNING, Bertie took some slops down to the pigs, and Jack was sitting around back by the garden going at his hoe with a sharpening stone. " 'Swallows for swallows,' " he muttered to himself, and kept at the hoe with smart strokes. Then to see him you might have thought he had a fit. He tossed the hoe aside and the stone up in the air and was on his feet before the stone fell and running around to the front of the cottage yelling out, "Bertie, Bertie, I got it, I got it! Bertie, Bertie, I got it!"

But Bertie was nowhere in sight. She was in a black bag on the back of a dark horse galloped by Zork's man toward the city, out of sight to Jack, over the hill, gagged and gone, no magic, but just a plain old kidnapping, or worse maybe.

Zork's man lugged the bag in the back way of the palace. He liked to keep his business secret, and had to cuff a room maid senseless to get around her and up to Zork's quarters unnoticed. He untied the bag and let it fall around Bertie. Zork made a mock bow to the lady. The man took off Bertie's gag.

"That was the most ungrateful thing that's ever happened to me!" Bertie said to Zork's man. "You come asking for directions and then stick a person in a bag when she's kind enough to help you. Don't ever ask again. I wouldn't tell you which way is up."

"Hold your tongue, woman," Zork commanded, "or I'll cut it out." He walked around Bertie, looking her over. He had a long storklike way about him, also a sharp nose and a scraggly little head that popped up through his red cape, as if he had squeezed his head small by bearing down too hard on tiny schemes. "Bring the loaf," he ordered his man. It was set down in front of Bertie.

"Do you recognize this?" Zork asked.

"Bread is bread," Bertie said. "It all looks alike to me."

"But this loaf of bread was a pig, and it was you that changed it into this loaf. I want to know how you did that."

Bertie laughed. "A story for a nitwit," she said.

"Cut her liver out," Zork said, jerking a finger at his man.

"Oh, no!" gasped Bertie. "You wouldn't do that, would you? Oh, my, I see you would." Zork's man had his knife out and was coming up to her. "I meant no harm—it was only because I was angry at that man knocking me in the ditch. I can change the loaf back into a pig if it's so important to you. It's only a little poem what does it."

"Yes," Zork said, waving his man away. "Do that, do that." He rubbed his hands together, eager to know such powerful words. Then he would have her liver cut out.

Bertie got herself free from the bag, making some unnecessary foolery out of it so she had a chance to get the blue stone from her pocket and slip it into her mouth. Then she stood in front of the loaf and said to it:

> *"The King is wise,*
> *and the Queen is pretty,*
> *and this poem might change*
> *a loaf to a piggy."*

And it did. Just like that.

"This trick I will do today before the King's eyes!" exclaimed Zork. "This is the best trick of all I've seen done! Now, woman, change it back into a loaf so I may take it to court."

Bertie thought it was unwise to do that, to give away all her magic to someone who talked so freely of cutting out her tongue and liver. So she said to him, "That is a different poem. And I won't tell you now, but I will go to court with you and stand behind a screen, and at the right time I'll tell you the poem that changes the pig back into a loaf, and then I'll leave."

Zork didn't care much for the idea. He didn't plan on letting Bertie live, but he knew he could always have her picked up afterwards, and then cut her liver out. So he agreed and most graciously sent word to the King and Queen that he would be honored to present them with a new trick that would delight and astound them.

They gathered at court, the King and Queen on their thrones and Zork before them with the pig on a small table that was dressed in a silk cloth. Behind the table was a screen, and behind the screen was Bertie. Zork's man waited outside the door with the black bag and a sharp knife. Bag, butcher, and bury Bertie was what was on his mind. Bertie peeked out through the screen. The King and Queen were dumpy and plain.

"Ahem!" said Zork. "Illustrious and magnificent sovereigns. Past many adventures, divers and strange to tell, from the mysterious East by dint of much personal sacrifice, expense, and danger, have I brought to this court—notwithstanding various and sundry entreaties from several great kings and princes elsewhere to have for their own enrichment and diversion this wondrous and awesome show of true sorcery—have I brought before your excellent Highnesses, as I have mentioned, a wholly extravagant, not to say incredible, and possibly appalling . . ."

"What are you going to do with the pig?" the King asked.

"Ahem. Well, sire, I was coming to that. I'm going to change it into a loaf of bread."

"It better be good," said the Queen, picking her teeth with a long fingernail.

"Yes," Zork said. "Yes, of course. A few magic words and presto!"

"Presto," the Queen said doubtfully. "Get on with it."

Zork then made a great show of swirling his cape around and waggling his fingers at the pig. Shielding himself from the King and Queen behind his cape, he stood by the screen and whispered to Bertie, "Now! Now is the time. Tell me the words."

And Bertie whispered back at him:

> *"The Queen is ugly,*
> *and the King is an oaf,*
> *and this poem might change*
> *a pig to a loaf."*

Zork dropped his arm and stood looking dumbly at the pig. "Er . . . ah . . . erk. . . ."

"It's still a pig," said the King.

"Er . . . ahk," said Zork.

"*Those* are magic words? You sound like there's a bone stuck in your gullet," the Queen said. "And who's that behind the screen there?"

Bertie stepped out and bowed low. "Only a simple country woman, your Majesty, but one who has enough sense to know you can't change a pig into a loaf of bread. But I can take it to the kitchen and make it into a fine roast, if it please your Highnesses."

"Well said," the King declared. "And as for you, Magician, you are banished forever. Begone! And take that big rat-eyed bully with you!"

Zork rushed out, happy to get away with his head, and within the hour both he and his man were off on their separate ways out of the kingdom forever.

Bertie directed the roasting of the pig but did not stay for compliments. The workers in the kitchen wrapped her some lunch in a clean towel, and she was on the road in a short time and scampering back toward home as fast as she could go.

Jack had looked for her at all the neighbors', and had been to see sister Minn, and wandered up and down the road asking strangers if they had seen Bertie. As a last resort he went to see the Old Magger who, although she was usually reluctant to help someone in need without good payment, showed a peculiar interest in the case. One of her pigs just the day before had come back to the pen with only three legs, and she sensed something worthwhile was happening, something that might be turned to dark, secret, and perhaps profitable purposes.

The Old Magger studied the ground where Zork's man

had trapped and bundled up Bertie. She prowled around, bent over at the waist, and gave her opinion.

"Rats and dungeons, Jack."

"What does that mean?"

"Nay, Jack, I can't tell you more." She had seen Bertie leading the gift pig down to sister Minn's, and now she glanced up into Jack and Bertie's slop pen and studied their new pig. "Where'd you get the new pig, Jack?"

But Jack wouldn't say. "I can't tell you that."

"Secrets, eh? Pig secrets, aye, there seems to be pig secrets about. Pig magic. Better tell, Jack, better tell the Old Magger. Three-legged pig magic, eh, Jack? Better tell the Old Magger, Jack." She crooned and took Jack by the belt. Jack broke away and ran off to the cottage.

"Snot!" said the Old Magger. She studied the new pig for a while and went back to her shack.

Jack was just leaving the cottage with a pack when Bertie came up the path. After kissing and hugging and crying a little, they sat and talked quietly about what had happened. "We was warned, Bertie," Jack said, "and maybe that's not the end of it." He had all the shutters closed, and now and then he went to the door and listened. Once he unbolted it quietly and flung it wide open. No one was there. "The Old Magger knows something, Bertie—we've got to be careful." Then in an even quieter voice, he told Bertie that he thought he'd learned something more out of the song about the blue stone. Come morning, they would test it out.

The Swallow

JACK walked in front of Bertie down the back path to the stream and came up to the exact spot where the stone had been found.

"There, Jack," said Bertie. "There ain't no birds, let's go back."

Jack looked at a nearby group of alders. He picked up a couple of rocks and sailed them into the trees. No birds. He shrugged.

"No matter. Give us the blue stone, Bertie."

"You're a fool, Jack. Suppose a bird does fly down and eats it and flies off? Then we've lost it completely, even if we only mean to make a nice pig when we need one. I promise I'll never use it for anything else, Jack."

" 'Swallows for swallows,' " Jack said. "That means that a swallow *bird* is supposed to swallow the stone. That's what it's for, Bertie. Human beings wasn't meant to find it in the first place, nor have it and own it once they know better. It's all in the song."

"But why, Jack. What good does it do a bird?"

"That ain't up to us to know, Bertie. All we got to do is follow the song. I almost lost my head, and you almost lost your liver for trying to make something out of it we shouldn't. Give us the stone, now."

"I never want to be such a half-wit as yourself, Jack," Bertie said, but handed him the stone.

Jack took and set it down in the grass near the stream bed. He led Bertie by the arm back behind some bushes to watch. He whispered, "Remember them birds all around when we found the stone, Bertie? They was swallows. My guess is that when these blue stones fall out of heaven, all the swallows around know about it and try to get to them. But this one fell in the water and they couldn't, and had to be happy with scolding me when I found it. Now we just wait and see."

"What do you suppose will happen, Jack?"

"Can't tell, Bertie. There's still some of the song I ain't figured out yet." He said the last two lines of the song:

> *"but swallows for swallows and wings for the new,*
> *born of the angels, the pieces are blue."*

And then in a while they saw the bird. They could tell it was a swallow a good distance off, seeing its split tail and pointed wings. It came straight to the stone in a glide and landed right next to it. Then it approached, took the blue stone in its beak and tilted its head back and let the stone drop down its throat.

And there!

"Good Lord!" cried Bertie. "It changed to a *baby*!"

It had. An infant child was lying in the grass on its back, and it started to cry. Bertie snatched her shawl off as she ran to it, and had it bundled up in a minute. The baby kept crying.

"The poor thing's hungry, Jack. Go quick to sister Minn's and get some cow milk—and a bottle and a nipple."

Jack ran off, and Bertie climbed the path to the cottage. She had the baby in a blanket and was trying to hush it by rocking and singing when Jack returned with a bottle of warm milk.

"Cow was near dry," Jack said. "Tomorrow we can have all we want."

"Mercy," said Bertie, giving the baby the bottle. "The little thing's so hungry, Jack."

"I wonder should we feed it, Bertie."

"Of course we should feed it," Bertie said crossly. "Would you let a baby cry and go hungry because it doesn't fit in with an old song? Hmmpf!"

Jack didn't have an answer to that.

"Oh, Jack, you ought to hold it. I'd never forget how it is, but every time it's just a feeling you can't remember enough about."

Jack fretted but tried not to get Bertie cross.

"Whose baby do you suppose it is, Bertie?"

Bertie looked at him sternly. "If you've got any ideas we're going to leave this baby out for the birds, Jack, you can put those ideas in that bucket and put your head in afterwards."

Those weren't Jack's ideas, and in fact he hadn't any good ideas. But he felt nervous about the baby, as if they were doing the wrong thing to keep it.

Presently the baby was finished with the milk, and Bertie laid it over her shoulder and burped it. After three hits it belched, and up came the stone and popped out of the baby's mouth onto the floor. When Bertie heard the stone hit the floor, she knew exactly what had happened, and she clutched the baby to her breast.

"It ain't changed, Jack, has it?" Bertie cried in anguish

87

and alarm. "It ain't a pig or anything is it, Jack?"

It wasn't. It was still the same baby.

"But let up on it, Bertie. You'll squeeze the thing to death!"

"Can't, Jack—got to hold it tight so it don't have a chance to change back into a bird or something. Oh, Jack! I can feel the dear thing trying to change back! Oh, Jack!" And she hugged the baby till it let out a grunt.

"Bertie! Bertie!" Jack cried, stepping around in front of her with his hands out wanting to do something to help. "Don't crush it so, Bertie! You'll break the little thing!"

Little by little, Bertie relaxed her hold but still clasped the baby good and firmly to her breast, and at last didn't dare let it go any farther, all the while asking Jack to watch it close if it showed any signs of wanting to change to anything else. Finally, Bertie was holding it just sort of snugged up close and could get a breath herself. She smiled and dared to pat the baby and hum to it, and it fell asleep.

"Bertie," Jack said, "now what are you going to do?"

"Look, Jack, it's sleeping. Isn't it the dearest thing you've ever seen? Oh, Jack, I won't stand for it changing back into a bird."

"You can't just hold it, Bertie."

"I've got to, Jack."

"How will you eat?"

"You can feed me, Jack."

"I can't sleep for you, Bertie. You've got to sleep."

"We'll see," said Bertie. She hummed to the baby. "All I know, Jack, is if I let it go it'll change into something else. I ain't going to let it happen, Jack."

Jack felt sure it was wrong but didn't say anything more. He put some stew together and fed Bertie with a spoon. When the baby woke up he made some sugar water for it. Bertie held the baby all day and was holding it when Jack went to bed.

"You've got to sleep, Bertie."

"We'll see," Bertie said.

The Old Magger

BERTIE was awake and cheerful in the morning.

"Go milk sister Minn's cow, Jack. The dear thing's hungry enough to eat my collar."

Jack went off to do that and returned with a bucket of milk. Bertie fed the baby.

"Ain't you tired, Bertie?"

"Never, Jack."

All day long Bertie sat in the chair with the baby, and she wouldn't let go to come to bed.

"You've got to sleep, Bertie."

"We'll see," Bertie said.

There were dark circles under Bertie's eyes the next morning. Jack watched her for hours. She wanted to talk and be talked to. She started talking about when she was just five years old and talked all day up to her tenth birthday. Jack worried for her. Now and then she started to nod, but as soon as her arms relaxed, she gripped up tight again and talked some more, sometimes droning off like she was half asleep. It came time for bed again.

"You've got to sleep, Bertie."

"We'll . . . see," Bertie said.

She was awake the next morning. This would be her fourth day without sleep. She looked old and very tired. Jack decided to take the baby from her. Once, when her talking about her nineteenth year trailed off, Jack got up and put a hand on the baby.

"Don't you do it, Jack," Bertie said, without opening her eyes, and Jack sat down again and worried. If Bertie didn't sleep, she would die right there in the chair. Jack concluded that he would have to go see the Old Magger to get some magic brew that would put Bertie to sleep. He told Bertie he was going out for a while and kissed her on the forehead. He walked on down, then, and took the pig that had been made from the loaf for payment to the Old Magger.

It was smelly with pigs and worse down by the Old Magger's shack. A thin tail of smoke was coming out of the stone chimney. Jack beat his fist on the door. The Old Magger peeked at Jack out of a side curtain, then came to the door.

"Hah!" she said, crooking a finger at Jack. "Pig magic. The pig magic man. I knew you'd come around, Jack. Heh, heh. Pig magic trouble. Them that don't know magic get in trouble with it, pig magic man. Heh, heh, heh, heh."

She was dressed in a large jacket with several pockets in it, most of them just sewed on patchwork, and all were full of little bottles and things wrapped up in paper, and scrummy little odds and ends she had gathered from the woods. A large black pot was over the fire, and in it was the three-legged pig, tied up and pouring off sweat from the heat. Jack walked round past that way and looked in on the curious affair. The pig was alive, but terribly hot and groaning, and the fumes were coming up around its head almost thick enough to choke it.

"Never mind that," snapped the Old Magger. "That's none of your business."

Actually, she was trying to put together a brew that would make some witchery fumes to make the pig talk and tell her how it had come to lose a leg so neatly. Once, years before, she had succeeded in an experiment like this with a cat. Almost, anyway. When she had put in the last ingredient and put another stick on the fire, the cat appeared to be ready to talk. At least it looked like it wanted to say something. But then it died.

Jack preferred not to sit down. He told the Old Magger that Bertie wouldn't go to sleep, and that what he needed was a sleeping potion to put in her tea. The Old Magger said that it could be done, but she wanted to know more.

"Why won't she go to sleep, Jack? Has it to do with pig magic?"

"I can't tell you more."

"Heh, heh, heh. People what doesn't go to sleep falls over dead, Jack. Tell us more, Jack."

And she kept at him, so that at last Jack had to tell her everything about the blue stone. He was too worried about Bertie to do anything else. And the Old Magger wanted to know everything, right from the beginning, every single thing since they first found it, and the song about it, and the pig poems, and everything that had happened. Jack told her all.

"And where's the blue stone now, Jack?"

"I don't know. On the floor I suppose. Do you have any of the sleeping potion already made up?"

"Nay, nay," said the Old Magger. "It isn't one you make up, Jack, but one of the kind that grows in the woods. It's a flower, a purple flower that has a closed eye in the middle of it, and you squeeze the juice of it into Bertie's tea and she'll sleep, Jack."

"Do you have some of these flowers?"

"Nay, but they can be got by yourself, Jack." She walked to the window and pointed to some hills in the distance. "See, Jack, see that middle hill off there? That's the one. You go on up there and you pick those little purple flowers near the top, and then Bertie can sleep."

Jack left immediately. "Heh, heh, heh, heh," the Old Magger laughed as she watched Jack hurry off. There were no purple flowers on that hill that she knew anything about, but the journey would get Jack out of the way for a long time. When he was ten minutes gone the Old Magger went up to the cottage and looked in the open door. "Bertie?" she said. "Are you sleeping yet, Bertie?"

Bertie turned in her chair. "What do you want here? Get away from here! Scat!"

"Heh, heh. What a darling baby. Is it yours, Bertie? Heh, heh." All the time she was looking around the floor for the blue stone.

"Get out of here! Get out!"

The Old Magger spied the blue stone on the floor, and put a foot in the doorway. "Is it a sweet baby, Bertie? Does it sing like a little bird? Heh, heh, heh." Then the Old Magger made a dash and plucked the stone off the floor and was back outside the door before Bertie could move.

"Get away from here!" Bertie shouted. "Get! Get!"

"Is it soft like it's got feathers all over it, Bertie? Heh, heh, heh."

Bertie stood up and came kicking at the Old Magger, and she ran off. Bertie kicked the door shut after her. The Old Magger scatted down the hill to her shack with the blue stone wrapped inside both hands.

The Last of the Song

JACK trudged around and across the crown of the hill the Old Magger had indicated to him but found no purple flower with a closed eye in the middle of it. Weary and bush-torn he returned, opened the door and found Bertie asleep in her chair, her head lolled back, and snoring. The blanket lay half across her back and half on the floor. Her arms hung limply at her sides. The baby was gone. Jack sank to his knees in exhaustion and relief and put his head in his hands. After a couple of minutes, he got up and moved to Bertie's side and held her head up.

"Bertie, darling, you'll sleep better in bed. Come on, Bertie."

"Huh? What? Huh?" Bertie came awake slowly, but when the slightest remembrance came to her she clutched at the blanket, and then cried out for the lost baby. Dropping to the floor, she moaned as she searched through the folds of the blanket, and then she wept, and Jack sat on the floor with his arms around her.

"Oh, Jack, I let it go, I let it go! Oh, Jack, and now the dear thing's just a bird again and has flown off. Jack, I'd rather have died than to let that happen."

"I know, Bertie, I know." Jack patted her. "I know, Bertie."

There came a noise from the bedroom. It sounded like something had bumped against the window, and before Jack or Bertie could get on their feet, the baby came out of the room.

"Oh, Lord, Jack," Bertie cried. "It's got wings!"

The baby was flying up near the ceiling. It took two turns over their heads. It was smiling and holding out its arms toward them. Then it flew out the open door and up into the sky. Jack and Bertie crowded to the door and watched it fly away, higher and higher, up higher than the clouds into the blue sky, flying with the rhythm of a swallow, its pointed wings carrying it strongly, and then they could see it no more.

Jack said, " 'Swallows for swallows and wings for the newborn of the angels . . .' "

"Lord!" breathed Bertie. "A baby *angel*!"

"And that's the last of the song," Jack said.

"Thank goodness," said Bertie. "I don't think I could stand any more."

Enough

THE NEXT DAY Jack said, "I'd best go down to the Old Magger's and get that stone back from her before she gets in any trouble with it."

"Do what you want, Jack, but throw it back in the stream. I don't want to see it no more. The working of heaven is enough to tire a person out completely."

"Aye, it is a strange way to have babies, ain't it, Bertie?"

"Roundabout, that's the word for it, Jack."

Jack went down to the Old Magger's and was back in a few minutes. "I thought she was home," Jack said. "Had her fire going. But when I got there I couldn't raise her. Heard some commotion inside so I looked through a window, but she wasn't there. Funny, she had some bread all set up for baking, half risen and ready to be punched down. Several loaves. But she wasn't in sight. Just some pigs in there chasing a chicken about. It flopped against the window like crazy, but I let it be. None of my business, and I wouldn't go in there without being asked." Jack mused for a bit. "Looked like them pigs was going to get that chicken, too."

"She can have the stone for all I care," Bertie said.

"Well, she knows the song about it, so I suppose anything that happens to her is her own fault."

"Aye," said Bertie. She was folding up the baby's blanket. "Jack?"

"Aye, darling?" He poured them both some tea.

"There wasn't much come of it after all, was there?"

"No gold, Bertie. No pig, either—not even a chicken or duck, finally." He set the tea out on the table for them.

"But you know, Jack, I believe it's a great blessing just to have an angel visit in your house."

"That's true, Bertie." He sipped his tea. "I suppose that's as much as there was to it."

And that's as much as there was to it.

It was enough.

It was plenty.

THE LEPRECHAUN'S STORY

Once I saw a leprechaun in the grass, his head in profile, perfectly formed: brow, cheek, chin, and neck. I smiled and said to myself, "How nice, that a mere clump of grass in the breeze and sun can take on the appearance of a small man. How wonderful the imagination is to accommodate such a creation." And as I looked, the little man turned his head and glanced at me, appraised my doubt, turned his head slowly away and disappeared. Then I was looking at a clump of grass, and there was no way to make it look like anything else.

In FAIR IRELAND there came along a country road a village tradesman, strolling at his ease and looking about to see what profit might come of it. He poked his cane about himself, thinking all the while how generous and lovely the world was to a fellow who was quick with his wits.

Presently he was walking alongside a hedgerow, and he heard a soft humming from the other side. So with care not to make a sound, he parted the branches to see the matter of it. And right there was sitting a leprechaun busy at making a pair of small soft boots, for leprechauns are cobblers to fairies, as you might know.

"Arrah!" cries the tradesman with a great shout, jumping through the hedge. "There ye be, ye little imp, and my eyes are right on ye till ye take me to the gold treasure!"

For that's the way it is if you come upon a leprechaun. If you keep your eyes on him and do not close them or look away, then he must take you to a gold treasure. But the leprechaun will try to trick you into looking away.

So the leprechaun looks up and says, "Faith, and it's the truth, I must take ye to the gold. But ye'll have no use for gold if ye don't look out for that tree that's about to fall on yerself."

"Bad luck to ye, leprechaun," says the tradesman. "D'ye think ye'll be tricking me so easy?" And he did not look around for any falling tree, but kept his eyes on the little man.

"Ye may be clever," says the leprechaun, "but not clever enough to keep that tiger from leaping on yer back."

"Och! and that's a feeble trick," says the tradesman. "There be no tigers in Ireland." And he did not look about for any tiger, but kept his eyes steadily on the leprechaun.

The little man glanced down the road. "Ah, and there's a glorious sight!" says he. "A prancing white horse and a bonny lass riding with her skirts blowing in the breeze."

"Ye come closer that time," says the tradesman. "Sure, and there are beauties in Ireland, but I'll not be looking at this one. Me eyes are right on ye."

"That they are," says the leprechaun. "Another stitch at my work and it's off to the gold with us." He put his attention to his work for a few moments as the tradesman watched him, and with a final snip he was done with the boots. "There!" says the leprechaun and stands up.

But on that moment he jumps backward and cries out, "God's mercy! The devil himself has popped up behind ye!"

"Aye?" says the tradesman. "And he may have reason. But away with yer tricks, me little darling. I haven't blinked me eyes since first spying ye, and now it's off to the gold with us."

"Sure, and there's no fooling ye this day," sighs the leprechaun, tucking his needles in his belt. "Aye, it's off to the gold. Do ye be ready for the journey?"

"Ready as yerself," says the tradesman. "And please yer tinyness, just walk in front where I can keep me eyes on ye."

So off they went—not on the roadway, but across the lovely green countryside.

Soon they came upon a rope bridge stretched over a small river, and the leprechaun crossed first, very carefully. As the tradesman was crossing the swinging bridge the leprechaun says, "Watch yer feet or ye'll be falling." But the tradesman crossed safely without taking his eyes off the little man.

A shallow lake stood in their way a short distance onward, and a flat-bottomed skiff was pulled upon the shore. Boarding it, the leprechaun handed the tradesman a pole and took one himself; then they proceeded to push themselves across the lake. In the center of the lake the skiff tipped dangerously to one side. The leprechaun cries out, "Look to yer pole or we'll go over!" But the tradesman stared at the leprechaun and the boat righted itself and they landed safely on the farther shore.

They came next to a small canyon. A rope was fastened to a high tree branch on which they could swing across. The leprechaun did so and landed lightly on the other side. He swung the rope back to the tradesman, who then pushed off from his side. "Watch the ground when ye drop off or ye'll be breaking a leg!" cries the leprechaun, but the trades-man keeps his eyes right on the little man and lands safely after all.

The last difficulty was a high cliff in their way. It was a dangerous ascent, and the leprechaun climbed slowly and carefully. When he was at the top, the tradesman began his climb. Many times the leprechaun called down to him to watch his hands and mind his feet, and to be careful for this and that loose rock, and to give him good advice regarding broken necks and cracked skulls. But still the tradesman would not take his eyes off the leprechaun, and finally he made it safely to the top. There they sat down and rested.

"Whew!" says the leprechaun. "Ye be a greedy man to go along so blindly in those dangers."

"Call it what ye will," says the tradesman. "And now for the gold, according to the rules."

"Aye," says the leprechaun, "and ye deserve it, the whole pot of gold. Yet it's very sad I am for the woman."

"What woman is that ye speak of?"

"The poor woman I was thinking to give the gold to before ye discovered me. So needy she is, and such a fine soul."

"Truth, and many people are poor," says the tradesman.

"Truth indeed," says the leprechaun, "but for this poor woman it's been just one misfortune against another. Close yer eyes and picture how it is with her while I tell ye the story of it."

"It's very well I can picture the story with me eyes open and looking right at ye."

"As ye say," says the leprechaun. "Well, she lives in a hut that's no more than a patch on the ground, and she has five children. Her husband was made blind when he was kicked in the head by the horse."

"Ah, that's a shame," says the tradesman. "But it's lucky he is to be alive, and a horse is always valuable."

"That it is, but the horse broke his leg when he kicked the man and had to be put out of his pain, ye know. Then the man went to walking into a well, and it was through for him in this world."

"But sure the poor family was left with a cow at least?" asks the tradesman.

"Faith, and ye might call it a cow," says the leprechaun. "It gave no milk and couldn't be turned with a switch or the name of any saint. The quare heathen beast wandered into the forest and was lost, but not until she attended to trampling the garden down."

"So the poor family hasn't a garden even?"

"It's grubs and roots for them now," says the leprechaun, "and sore hungry the children are. The oldest is only eight. None have shoes, and the baby hasn't any clothes at all."

"Pitiful," says the tradesman, taking a handkerchief out and touching the corner of his eye. "I was a poor lad meself."

"Then ye have the heart to understand. The baby crawls on the filthy floor when the poor woman is out digging grubs, and it's terrible the way the rats go at him, and the other children just sit about crying from hunger."

"But sure they have a dog to catch the rats?"

"They have, but he's got only three legs and is no use for it."

"God's toes, it's a sad story," says the tradesman, blowing and wiping his nose.

"Is yer own dear mother alive?" asks the leprechaun.

"No, and God rest her soul."

"Aye, it's like yer own sainted mother this woman is," says the leprechaun. "The children are starving away before her eyes, sick most often now in want of money for a doctor to attend their fevers."

The tradesman began to weep softly.

"And think of it," says the leprechaun. "Yer own self will soon have a whole pot of gold."

The tradesman sniffled. "Aye, 'tis a strange world indeed."

The leprechaun nodded. "And them so needy for only a single gold piece."

"Aye," said the tradesman, blowing his nose. "There's no understanding it."

"Now it's all yer own fair winnings," says the leprechaun. "Yet there's a favor I'd be asking ye."

"And what is that?" sobs the tradesman.

"So very little they have," says the leprechaun. "And the poor woman is so weak she can't raise the axe to chop wood. Last of all they sold their cooking pot. Now the children must eat their grubs raw and cold."

"Och, the poor woman, the poor children!" the tradesman sobs out.

"For the favor then," says the leprechaun. "D'ye suppose that when ye take the gold ye could leave the pot for the poor family to cook their grubs in?"

"God's name!" bawled the tradesman. "It's the saddest

story I've ever heard. Merciful heaven, let's leave them the pot!"

And he was so overcome by the plight of the poor family and his own charity that he began to weep in fullness, and he buried his face in his hands and shook with sobbing.

A few moments later when he looked up, the leprechaun was gone. Then the tradesman realized that the little man had made up the story. There was no poor woman, no hungry children, no rats and no three-legged dog. It was all a trick to make him cry and look away from the leprechaun. So the tradesman put his face into his handkerchief again and bawled more than ever before.

THE CONTESTS
AT COWLICK

I was writing a story about a bell in a church steeple that was broken and didn't ring. It happened long ago, in Europe some-where, and barbarian raiders arrived to sack and pillage the town, and the bell had to ring to call for help, but could not ring loud enough. The story got stuck at this place, and would not move until I set it in the Wild West, dressed the barbarian chief in a ten-gallon hat and six guns, and sent the sheriff off fishing.

HOGBONE and his gang rode into the little town of Cowlick one dusty afternoon when the sheriff and his men had gone fishing.

"If you need us," the sheriff said as they left, "we'll just be a holler up the creek."

So when the townsfolk saw Hogbone and his gang coming they hollered for the sheriff and his men. First the mayor hollered. Then the baker. Then the barber. Then several others tried it, and the banker hollered loudest of all. But when the sheriff and his men did not come, the townsfolk ran off to hide.

The streets were empty, doors latched, and windows locked as Hogbone and his gang rode up the main street. Here and there an eyeball showed at a knothole or between boards, and shadows moved with cat slowness behind cur-tains.

Hogbone and his fifteen men pulled up their horses in

front of the bank. For the looks of it, Cowlick might have been a ghost town.

"Hey!" Hogbone yelled out. "Where's all the chickens in this coop? Hah?—how about it? Where's your sissy sheriff and his girlfriends? Bring 'em out so we can shoot 'em for a while!"

The shadows froze on the curtains, and not an eyeball showed.

"Well, shucks! This ain't no fun," Hogbone complained. "Heck! Well, go git the money, boys." Scratching and spitting, some of the men got down off their horses. "Heck!" Hogbone said again. "I was looking for a little trouble."

At this moment Wally crawled out from under a horse trough and stood before the Hogbone gang.

"If you want some trouble," said Wally, "I can give you some trouble."

Hogbone dropped a look on the boy and said, "Most trouble you'd give me is stickin' between my teeth when I chaw you up."

"Har, har, har!" laughed the gang.

"Shut up!" said Hogbone.

"I'm the fastest runner anywhere around here," said Wally. "I bet I can win a footrace with your five best men."

"Well, ain't that a pretty how-de-do? I just reckon we might use a little fun." And Hogbone called out, "Alligator, Blackwhip, Snakebite, Gouge-eye, Crumby—git down here and do a little leg-stretching."

The men got down off their horses and Wally drew a line in the dust.

"We'll race down to the end of the street, around the

corner and into McGee's Livery Stable," said Wally, getting down on the line. The five men hitched up their pants and kicked their spurs off, sailed their hats out of the way and dropped their gun belts. They hunched down on the line with Wally.

"Ready?" Wally said.

"Ready," the men grunted.

Hogbone held up his forty-four. "On your marks—get set—" BLAM!

The runners jolted across the line. Wally ran last—all the way down the street, and he was the last one around the corner. Some townsfolk came out of hiding as the runners raced by.

When Wally got to McGee's Livery Stable all five men were inside, laughing at him as he jogged up to the door. Wally smiled and slammed the heavy door on them and bolted it shut. He walked slowly back to Hogbone and the remaining ten men of the gang. A few more townsfolk were standing timidly about on the dusty street.

"They beat me," said Wally. "They got a drink and sprawled out in the straw."

"Har, har!" laughed Hogbone.

"Har, har, har!" laughed his men.

"Shut up!" growled Hogbone.

"I got a bad start or I could have beat them," Wally said. "So that didn't count much. But I'll give you another try. Pick five men and I bet I can climb faster than any of them."

"You're a sassy little mouse," said Hogbone. "What you need is a good whupping, and I got the men to do it." And he called out, "Horseblanket, Saddlehorn, Cinch, Rake-spur, Yankbit, git over here!"

The five men got over there, grinning as they dropped their gun belts, took off their spurs and tucked at their shirts. More townsfolk came out to watch.

"We'll need two long ladders set up against the side of the church," said Wally. Some big boys ran off and got two twenty-foot ladders and set them up. Everyone stood around as Wally called out the rules of the contest. "Now, you five men go up that ladder and I go up the other one, and I mean to beat you all to the top and sit on the roof of the church first."

"This ought to be good," said Hogbone. "We might even have a neck-breaking." And he raised his forty-four.

BLAM!

The climbers jumped at their ladders and clambered up.

All five men were up and across the roof and sitting on the ridgepole of the church before Wally was even at the top of his ladder. He stopped climbing and looked down. More townsfolk had come out of hiding to watch the contests. Some were carrying guns.

"Darn!" said Wally, looking up to the men on the roof above him. "You guys sure are good climbers."

"You ain't bad yourself for a sprout," said Horseblanket.

Wally yelled down to Hogbone. "They beat me fair, but I got one other contest I know I can beat those last five men at."

"Come on down off there, ya little rooster, and I'll give you a last chance," Hogbone yelled back.

Wally turned to the men on the roof again. "I'll bet you guys could outclimb a mountain goat."

"Ain't bad yourself, for a kid," said Saddlehorn.

"You guys comfortable up there? Can you see pretty good?" Wally asked.

"Just fine," said Rakespur.

"Best seat in the house," said Yankbit.

"It's a cinch," said Cinch.

So Wally left them on the roof and climbed down. By now there was a good crowd of townsfolk standing around.

"I know I don't look so strong," said Wally to Hog-bone.

"Ya look like my little bitty sister," said Hogbone.

"Maybe so," Wally said, "but I can lift my horse over there." He pointed to a small pinto tied to a rail.

"I gotta see that," said Hogbone, "even if he is a runt horse."

"Okay," Wally said, "then it's a contest. I bet you I can lift my horse and I bet your five men there can't lift those big pigs they're riding."

Hogbone got red in the face and yelled, "Bump, Stump, Crump, Dump, Lump—git over here with your big—with your horses!" The men gathered around with their horses and Wally brought his pinto over.

"Now if you never lifted a horse before I can tell you it's a bit tricky," said Wally. "You have to get right underneath and lift straight up. Trouble is, the horse wants to slide off your back. So what you have to do is tie him on real tight. Here, get underneath your horses and I'll show you how it's done. Some of you people give a hand here," he said to the townsfolk.

Wally took a lasso from Bump's horse and tied it around over the top of the saddle and around under Bump's belly, and he took several loops like that and knotted the rope tight.

"That's how it's done," said Wally. The other men were tied under their horses the same way, tight up so just their feet and the tips of their fingers touched the ground.

"You sure got some pretty funny ideas," said Hogbone, studying the men under their horses.

"Pretty funny," said Wally. Then he walked over to the church and pulled both ladders away, and they slammed to the ground.

"Hey!" Yankbit shouted from the roof. "How we gonna git down from here?"

Right about then Hogbone began to catch on. He looked down the street where his runners had disappeared, then to the men on the roof, and then to the men tied underneath their own horses. He took out his forty-four and pointed it right between Wally's eyes. The townsfolk began to catch on, too, and a couple of the men pointed their rifles at Hogbone.

Wally spoke: "Now five of your men are locked in McGee's Livery Stable, and five are stuck on the church roof, and five are tied underneath their horses, and it looks like you can't do much alone."

"I can blow your head off," snarled Hogbone.

"Won't do you any good," said Wally, looking toward the men with rifles. "My friends here won't like that. Besides, you can have your men back and all the money in the bank if you can holler louder than me."

"Har, har!" laughed Hogbone. "A hollering contest? You think I got to be boss of this gang for nothing?"

"Har, har, har!" laughed his men.

"Shut up!" shouted Hogbone. The men shut up.

"You holler first," said Wally.

Hogbone scratched his chin and looked around very carefully. Then he shrugged and stuck his gun away in his holster.

"Okay," he said, "give me some air-sucking room." He spread his arms out and everyone moved back. Then he took a great breath of air and let out a holler.

"WHOOOOOOOOOOOOOOOOOOOOOOOOOOOOAAAA-AAAAAAAAA!"

"Pretty good," said Wally, "but I can holler louder. You've got to bring it way up from deep in the stomach."

"You think I don't know that?" said Hogbone. "Listen. YOWWWWWWWWWWWWWWWWWWWWWWWW-WWWWWWWWWWOOOOOOOOOOOOOOOO!"

"Not bad," said Wally, "but I can do better. If you took off your gun belt you could get more wind."

"That's a fact," agreed Hogbone, and he dropped his gun belt aside.

"HAAAAAAAAAAAAAAAAAAAAAAAAAAAAAA-AAAEEEEEEEEEEEEEEEEEEEEYYYYYYYYYYY!"

"Take off your hat and toss your head back more," Wally suggested.

On his sixth try, Hogbone's hollers were still improving. On his seventh try the sheriff and his men, who had been just a holler up the creek, rode up quietly behind Hogbone and took him by the arms. Hogbone was so winded from hollering that he didn't even put up a fight when the sheriff hauled him off. The rest of the gang were rounded up and clapped in jail with him.

As Wally passed the jail window Hogbone glared out at him.

"Pretty funny," Hogbone snarled.

"Har, har, har!" laughed his men.

"Shut up!" said Hogbone.

Then Wally got together his fishing gear and headed up the creek.

SONG OF THE HORSE

At the fairgrounds one day I came upon a young girl sitting cross-legged in front of an open stall, wherein stood a horse, equally as still as she. I stood several paces behind. The scene was like an altarpiece, like an icon, she like a priestess before an object of worship, so quiet but yet with a holy intensity that might have caused a universe to be created at any moment. This is what came of that privileged vision.

OUT of the house I go and down the hill. The sun shines on the green meadow, yellow flowers, blue sky, white clouds and brown path as I run to the center of all the world of color, the small red barn. And inside there, in the dim light, is a horse who is the center, the focus, the very heart of all horsedom, and he belongs to me. He is waiting for me. He is always waiting for me, standing still and thinking about me. Standing upright in his sleep he dreams about me, and he never dreams of anything else. Or if he does, he doesn't remember it. There is a picture of me inside his head that never goes away. Ever and always I am on his mind. Hardly anything is real to him but me. I think it a wonder that a horse can be so single-minded.

When he looks over the top of his stall into the sky, he sees my face in the clouds. He sees me in rainbows and shadows and hears my voice in the rain and the wind. The light of my eyes is in the stars, sun and moon. And now he sees me coming to him, and he snorts. That is his name for me. Now he blows through his lips, saying that he is ready to run, and he stomps his feet and runs his chest against his gate. He can hardly wait.

We stand face-to-face and I touch his nose. We look at each other. Spirit is his name. I say, "Spirit." He snorts my name again. It is the only name he knows, the name of all names to him—the name of apples and soap, of oats and clear water, of brushing his mane, the feel of my hand at his mouth, my gripping legs on his ribs. There is no name but me.

I open his gate and go into his stall. I put an arm over his neck as I reach for the bridle and reins. He shivers and moves. Naturally he is excited. He spends his life waiting for these moments. I must be careful he doesn't step on my foot.

"Easy, now," I say, patting him. One of us must remain calm.

O chest of Spirit, O neck, O mane, O jaw and belly and rump and tail. I loop his head with the rein. O leg and hoof of Spirit, O smell and power of Spirit.

"Open your mouth for the bit, you big dummy!"

Out we go and I swing onto his bare back. No horse and no rider have ever balanced so perfectly as Spirit and myself. I could ride him blindfolded, standing up, on one foot, tiptoe, with my arms outstretched. I think I could anyway. We walk, and this is a difficult time for him. We cannot run until we pass the gate, and he can hardly stand it.

He loves me to be on his back and he barely walks straight for nervousness and excitement. He loves the feel of my hands on his neck, the weight of my body, and the touch of my heels. Sometimes I don't understand how he can love me so much. Sometimes I think it is a kind of craziness.

His sides are like breathing mountains and he blows through his nose like a locomotive. His legs are like mighty wheels that have been made straight, his tail like spouting steam, and his eyes are like shining lights. We are almost at the gate. All his nerves are like the trembling strings of a great instrument. He waits for my touch to run, walking almost sideways for joy and eagerness. And here is the gate.

"Go!" I yell and slap his neck and dig my heels at his heaving sides and grip my knees to his ribs.

And we go!

O, my explosion of a horse; O, my lovely, heavenly horse; O, my God who made my horse and me! Ears like wands, hoofs like diamonds, breath like a volcano, mane like a storm in my face, we charge into the wind with our mouths open. We eat and drink the wind, we live on speed and thunder, we see by lightning flashes, and our charging gives birth to hurricanes and tornadoes. All underground creatures think we are an earthquake.

Moles and mice rush from their holes to see what great event is happening, but we are gone. We are a phantom, a ghost. We are wonderful to all things, beautiful to the earth, happy to all things, and the sound of our running is like a shout of wonder and awe. We run so fast that the trees look forever different after we pass. Fence posts are struck dumb by our speed. People who see us remember us only in dreams. The sheep argue about our existence. The slow-eyed grazing cows say we are fictional. The chickens think we are supernatural.

Faster and faster—and we are as close as clasped hands,

sharing each other completely, our pounding flesh and flash-ing blood, striking bones and beating brains—crossing and weaving ourselves together, knowing all of each other we ride madly into secrets and leave the shreds of mysteries behind us like a wake.

We lick the earth like a dark flame. All things know themselves as we approach and forget themselves as we pass. Nothing is the same forever after when the dust has settled behind us. Every blade of grass and clod of dirt remembers us, and the dust talks to the dust and tells stories and legends of our passing. Beetles and crickets think we are God.

All along the dreadful trail of our passing we leave the worship of horses. Distant hills and fields adore us and despair they have not the indelible print of our feet on their great slow bodies. And we run faster yet, a gigantic and vanishing sight.

We know everything! What we hear is all there is to hear. The rushing wind and the voice of the earth tell us all there is to tell. Thigh and bone, muscle and the rising heat of flesh and blood. We feel all there is to feel. We are the center of all senses. We see faster than the speed of light. The shouting and cheering world surrounds us all about. Faster, faster!

We run past the wind, past the shouting of praises, past the cheering and into stillness, past sound and into silence. We run past time and age and we run past our running and into slow motion. We run as in a dream—lifted away from our senses, frozen and flying in the heart of a crystal ball—and everything is revealed. I have no sisters, I have no brother. There is no barn and no house up the path, and

I have no mother or father. We run into a place where all is perfectly still, and there is no difference in anything and no sameness in anything, and in this great empty moment, a song is singing.

The song has words that are ancient and strange, and music like newborn water, tumbling all together, but I can't remember any of it. It is entirely beautiful. There is not too little of it and not too much. Nothing is left over. It is all perfect.

Sometimes my heart beats to the rhythm of it, and then I stop what I am doing and stand perfectly still, trying to hear the words and music of it. But I can't.

Only when I ride Spirit do I hear that song. Sometimes I fear I'll never hear it again.

Then comes an explosion, and we are overtaken by the sound of pounding hoofs, and we are back in time and slowing down. Wet and steaming, walking and panting, we go back to the barn.

I dry Spirit and comb him and feed him and talk to him. He hates to see me go. He is never tired of being with me. When I shut his gate he stares at me with a long look in his eyes, and he talks to me. I hear it in my mind. He says, "If you do not come back I will die of sorrow. I will not eat or sleep or open my eyes ever again, but I will lie down and breathe slower and slower until I stop breathing, because I could never live without you."

Then I put my cheek against his face and hold his great head and say to him, "Oh, Spirit." It comforts him.

I go out of the barn and walk up the path to the house. When I turn, he is looking at me. "No one will understand," he says, and shakes his head from side to side. And I walk away. I am sad because everything will be boring to him until I return, and he can't tell anyone how he feels. I stop for a moment on the path, listening, but I hear nothing. Then I go into the house.

Mother says to me, "Are you hungry?"

"I don't know," I say. "I guess so." I sit down and look out the window.

"Did you take Spirit for a run?"

"Uh-huh."

"Did you enjoy yourself?"

"It was all right."

THE RISE
AND FALL
OF
BEN GIZZARD

I was on my hands and knees, never mind why, looking through my legs, and the "V" of my crotch looked like a mountain upside down, and I remembered an old Indian at a watering hole telling me that he was looking for a man he was going to kill for doing him wrong, but he hadn't found the man yet, but he would, and he'd cross more mountains to find him, and he assured me that I wasn't him. Some stories are just given to you.

BEN Gizzard's mule coughed up blood in the morning, and Ben knew it was dying, so before sunset he traded the doomed beast to an old Indian for a bundle of furs. Ben squatted near the Indian's fire and told some lies to make the deal, which came natural to him, like being ugly. As he was making set to leave, the old Indian threw out a handful of sticks onto the ground and studied the future of the universe in them. He told Ben how he was going to die.

"A white mountain and a black bird," said the old man.

"What's that?" grunted Ben, hitching up a strap on his pack.

The Indian stared at the pattern of sticks. "The day will come when you will see a white mountain upside down, and just then a black bird will talk to you. On that day you will die."

Ben laughed, tossed the furs over his shoulder, and took to the trail again. Ben had no use for Indian witchcraft or anything else he couldn't lay his hands on. He was a shrewd trader and a mean man, and he figured a fellow could get along just fine in the world if he kept watching things out of the corners of his eyes. Ben's eyes had grown long and narrow over the years. He could stand in one spot and look right around the corner of something good, and right behind it, and see the bad part of it.

When he walked into Depression Gulch a few days later, he stuck up a tent and began looking around for someone to take advantage of. The sides of the gulch came right down to the main street, which was nothing but tents and a few shacks. Everyone was mining silver. The gulch was so narrow and high that the sun didn't come up till ten in the morning, and it set at two in the afternoon, but when it gave that narrow treeless alley some light, the outcroppings of silver on the sides of the gulch shone like fillings in a dark mouth, and the mines went in like cavities. Ben examined some of the digs and traded some furs for a claim a widow had, then swindled her out of her dead husband's tools and got to work.

There was silver yet in the diggings, and Ben swung his pick in the small mine. He worked for a week before the mine caved in on him. But by great luck a beam fell and stuck right above him, protecting him from the smothering fall of dirt and rocks. He waited in his small pocket of air and listened to the rescuers digging toward him. Ben wondered at his good luck to be alive. He remembered what the old Indian had said, that he would not die until the day he saw a white mountain upside down, and a black bird talked to him. You could see no mountain from the bottom of Depression Gulch, and no birds lived in the place. Ben wondered about this, lying there in the dark with his eyes open.

Ben kept working at his mine. It was just a week later when he had another close call. Ben and some other men were hanging around a dynamite shack when it blew up. Three men were killed in the explosion, but Ben wasn't even hurt. Even as he was flying through the air toward the bush that would gently catch him, Ben remembered what the old Indian had said about the white mountain and the black bird. He landed without a scratch.

That night Ben lay in his blankets and wondered some more. Twice he should have been killed, but he got out of it. What if the fortune the old Indian told was true? If it was, treeless, birdless Depression Gulch might be a very good place for a man like Ben Gizzard. If the old Indian *had* seen into the future and seen truly, then Ben could be as reckless as he wanted. He could cheat and swindle without a worry of being hanged or shot for it, and take any sort of chance to get above everybody else. The day would not come to Depression Gulch when he would die for his wickedness. Ben began waiting for one more proof of it.

The proof soon came. Two days later Ben was in the silver assayer's office when eight robbers rode into Depression Gulch and began shooting their way through town. They ripped up tents, shot out windows, set fires, loaded up with silver and killed anyone in their way. When they reached the assay office, Ben stepped out with two borrowed six-guns and faced them. Standing very still and quiet, with the robbers' bullets flying all around him, Ben took slow and careful aim and shot every single robber off his horse, one by one. Ben stood there in perfect health and watched them getting dragged off to the undertaker's by their boot heels. He looked up and around the town. Not a mountain in sight, not a bird.

That day, Ben Gizzard was made sheriff, and thereafter Depression Gulch was safe from all robbers except Ben Gizzard himself. He began bossing the town and making up laws. He got an office and started getting rich by making up laws and fining the people for breaking them. He set up a bank and made himself president of it. He built a courthouse and made himself judge, and got richer by stealing property and goods legally in trials. The town grew, and Ben held an election for mayor. He won the job because no one dared to run against him. When Ben had trouble with anybody, he found a weak excuse and simply shot him down. He never got hurt himself. There were no birds in Depression Gulch, and no mountains to be seen. Naturally, the townsfolk were afraid of a man so powerful who seemed to be charmed against any harm.

Now it was Mayor Ben Gizzard. Ben dressed himself in fancy hand-tooled boots, a beaver hat, fine suits and linen shirts with ruffles at the cuffs. He wore a diamond stickpin and tucked a gold watch in his vest pocket. He carried a silver-knobbed ebony walking stick with which he pushed open doors, rapped heads, and walloped dogs who came sniffing at him.

Ben gave his sheriff's badge to a scarred-up villain who only needed a little violence now and then to keep him relieved and happy. Together, they walked around town causing mischief and misery. Ben would hitch up his pants in satisfaction after a good swindle and say to his sheriff, "I guarantee you I ain't wearing silk shorts because I'm stupid." He used to say that quite often. He was proud of his silk shorts. They reminded him how smart he was. Even the ladies in town wore cotton. That was one of the laws.

There was also a law which the townsfolk considered stranger than the rest. It was this: No books with pictures in them were allowed in town. That was an easy law to keep, so Ben never collected any money on it. That's why the townsfolk thought it strange. But Ben had a good reason for it. He now fully believed what the old Indian had said to him, and he was making certain that there should not even be a *picture* of a white mountain in town. For if such a picture were in a book, then there would always be the chance that Ben might see that book open and upside down at that page. There were no white mountains to be seen, and no birds at all in Depression Gulch. And so what other men dared not do for fear of dying, Ben Gizzard would dare. Ben was perfectly safe to do as he pleased any day, since he would not die on that day, and he could not see forward to the day that he would. The town grew, and Ben became rich. He slid around town like a salamander in his silk shorts, and the cheated townsfolk looked on him with envy, hatred, and fear. Thus was the rise of Ben Gizzard.

One day when the sun was between the cliffs of Depression Gulch, Mayor Ben Gizzard looked out his office window and saw a young man walking into town. He had a pack on his back with a shovel sticking out of it. Ben's heart jumped when he saw him, for perched on the shoulder of the young man was a large black bird. He called out the door to the sheriff, and the two men strolled into the street. They cut into the young man's path and blocked his way.

"Howdy, I'm the mayor," said Ben.

"Hello, my name is Paul," said the young man. The black bird turned his head slowly and looked at Ben with its ancient reptilian eyes, then looked away disdainfully.

"You figure on staying long?" asked Ben. The sheriff circled around the young man, looking him up and down. Paul had no gun.

"I thought I might work some tailings for a bit," Paul said.

Ben nodded. After the mines and sluice boxes were worked there were heaps of discarded earth that contained tiny bits of silver. Those heaps were called tailings, and the miners allowed bums and drifters the small silver they held if anyone wanted to take the trouble to sift it out. It didn't amount to much. Ben looked at the black bird again. He put a fist up and shoved at it. The bird fluttered a wing out to keep its balance, but didn't even look at Ben. Paul frowned, but said nothing.

"Okay," said Ben. "Just watch yourself." He and the sheriff walked back inside.

Ben sat alone at his desk, watching the young man go up the street. He would have found some excuse to shoot him, but the young man appeared so mild and harmless it would have been difficult to give even a poor reason for it. "Well," he mused, rubbing his chin, "a dumb black bird is all, and no mountains around here. I can chase him out anytime." And he tried to forget about it.

Paul found an old abandoned shack and set it up for his

home. Then he got to working on the tailings. His black bird sat on his shoulder as he worked. He didn't work much, only a couple of hours a day, just enough to buy his food, and he seemed innocent of any intent except to lead a peaceful life. But Ben Gizzard kept an eye on him and the black bird.

Paul built a small porch on his shack, and got himself a stove. Blue smoke wove up out of the dark gulch above his place. High up where the smoke flattened out in the wind that swept across Depression Gulch, his black bird flew in wide, soft circles. Each day Ben Gizzard sent the sheriff around to the shack when Paul was in the tailings, and he got his reports.

"What's he up to?" Ben asked.

"Nothing. Just living quiet, far as I can see."

"Okay," said Ben. "Why don't you stick your feet up on the desk and relax." He poured the sheriff and himself a drink and tried not to worry about it.

But one day the report was different.

"What's he up to?" Ben asked.

"Painting a picture in there," the sheriff said, sticking his feet up on Ben's desk.

"Yeah? What kind of picture?"

"Mountain," said the sheriff.

Ben jumped to his feet. "Snow-covered mountain?"

"Yeah, so it is."

Ben took a swing at the sheriff's boots. "Get your stinking feet off my desk!" he yelled. The man stumbled to the door.

"Sorry, Mr. Gizzard! Sorry!" said the sheriff, all confusion, looking around the doorjamb. Ben was standing with his fists on his desk, grinding his teeth. The sheriff hoped to please him with something else he had found out. "Something else you ought to know, mayor," he said.

"What's that?" snarled Ben.

"He ordered some silk at the Wells Fargo station."

Ben slung a bottle at the man, who jerked his head away just in time. Mayor Ben Gizzard sat down at his desk and bit his fingernails for a while, then stuck his hat on and headed up toward Paul's shack. The door was open. Paul heard Ben come up on the porch.

"Come on in," the young man called out cheerily. Ben ducked his head through the door and went inside. Paul had an easel set up in the center of the room. The black bird was perched on top of it. On the easel was a scrap of old tent canvas nailed to a board, and on it was a painted picture of a perfect cone-shaped white mountain. Ben shot a glance at the bird, which returned the look scornfully and looked out the window.

"Hello, Mayor."

"What's that you're painting?"

"Mountain," said Paul. "Of course it ain't much on this old scrap of canvas, but I ordered some silk to paint it on."

"There ain't no mountain around here," said Ben. "How come a mountain?"

"I dream about it," said Paul, touching his brush gently to the canvas. "I close my eyes to remember it. It's beautiful, just so perfect and smooth and lovely. Of course this canvas is worn and rough, but when I get some silk you'll see how it really should look."

"There ain't going to be no silk," said Ben. "And there's

a law in this town that people can't paint dreams. It's a hanging law. Now you understand that?"

"Hanging?" said Paul, looking at the mayor. "You hang people for painting things they see in dreams? I never heard of such a law. And I can't have any silk to paint on? Is that a law, too?"

"That's right," said Ben, taking a slithering hitch on his trousers. "Since you didn't know the law, I won't hang you, but I'm taking that painting for evidence in case you break the law again."

Paul began to argue. Ben shoved him aside and walked over to the easel. He grabbed the painting. But he grabbed too quick and fumbled. The painting fell. It turned in the air as it fell toward the floor. In that astounding second Ben Gizzard could see that it was going to land upside down to him, and out of the wide and watching corner of his eye he saw that the black bird had jerked its head toward him and opened its beak as if to speak. Terror drove through Ben like a spike. Before the painting hit the floor, Ben clamped his eyes shut and slapped his hands over his ears and blundered out the small door and fell down the porch steps. He ran all the way back to his office and sat sweating at his desk, shaking all over, for he was certain that he had barely escaped his death for seeing a white mountain upside down and hearing a black bird talk to him.

After he had recovered he sent the sheriff up to get the painting. He ordered the man to take it by force, then burn it. The sheriff was back in the mayor's office in a half hour.

"Did you do it?" Ben asked.

"Yup," said the sheriff.

"Put your feet up on the desk and relax," said Ben.

"Sure," said the man. He looked curiously at the mayor and said, "I suppose you got a reason for me doing that?"

Ben hitched his trousers. "I guarantee you I ain't wearing silk shorts because I'm stupid," he said. Yet that night Ben slept poorly, and in the morning he was worried. He sent the sheriff up to Paul's shack for a report.

Ten minutes later, the sheriff returned. "Just painting," he said, tossing his feet up on the mayor's desk.

"What's he painting?" Ben asked.

"Another white mountain, that's all," said the sheriff.

"Get your stinking feet off my desk!" the mayor yelled. The sheriff started for the door, but Ben called him back to sit down. He reached for the bottle and poured each of them a drink, then said, "You know anything about birds?"

"Little."

"Can a black bird talk?"

"Some say so. Raven can anyway. Ravens are holy Indian birds. Indians say they talk all the time."

"That black bird that Paul's got up there—is that a raven?"

"Yup," said the sheriff.

Ben took another drink. "When does Paul come back to his shack?"

" 'Bout an hour," said the sheriff. Ben nodded. "Stick your feet up and relax. Here, have another drink." The sheriff was pleased to do both. He tilted his hat back and smacked his lips at the whiskey.

"When he comes back to the shack," Ben said, "kill him! Kill the bird, too."

The sheriff went back up to the shack when Paul returned. He pretended to visit and admire the painting. When he left he closed the door and put a wedge on it from the outside to trap Paul inside. Then he set the place on fire. But it was a bad job. Paul had a bucket of water handy. He put out the fire and climbed out the window with his bird.

The sheriff came back to the mayor's office and told what had happened. Ben cussed him and decided he'd have to help out with the job himself.

Early the next morning Ben took the sheriff off with him to Paul's shack while Paul was working at the tailings. Directly above the shack was an overhanging cliff with a great boulder balanced on it. Ben told the sheriff to climb up there and drop a string down with a rock on the end of it. The rock dangled directly above the porch, just outside the charred front door. Ben got his man with him again and gave orders.

"You stay up there with the boulder. I'll come around after Paul gets back from the tailings and get him to come out the door. Then I'll look up and nod at you, and you shove the boulder over the cliff. Got that?"

The sheriff nodded. "That's mighty smart, Mr. Gizzard."

"I guarantee you I ain't wearing silk shorts because I'm stupid. Now get up there!"

An hour later, Paul was in his shack painting when Mayor Ben Gizzard came around. Ben stood on the porch steps and greeted Paul in a friendly way, but Paul looked at him suspiciously. Ben squinted through the door. He could see a painting of a snow-covered mountain on the easel. The black bird was perched in its usual place on top of the easel.

It glanced at Ben with a cold and weary eye, then looked out the open window.

"Say, painting another mountain, are you?" said Ben, for he had to seem friendly to lure Paul outside onto the porch where the boulder would fall.

"You can't hang me for painting this one, Mr. Gizzard. This one's not a dream mountain. This one's real." Paul spoke a word to the black bird. It jumped from the easel and flew out the window. Up it circled, up and up until it rode high above Depression Gulch in the free wind. "Way up there my bird sees a real mountain," said Paul, "and he tells me about it, and this is a picture of that mountain."

Ben laughed, "That a fact? Talking bird, eh?" His voice was nervous.

"Yes, sir," said Paul, and he touched at the canvas with his brush.

"Well, Paul, that's great. I wouldn't want to stop you from painting that mountain. I been thinking it over and conclude we need a painter in town. Yes, I been thinking about just that. So you just step out the door here and I'll swear you in and make it all official."

Paul stopped painting and turned to the mayor. "I don't believe you, Mr. Gizzard. You tried to stop me painting once before and I think you tried to burn me out of here. I don't believe you like me at all. You shoved my bird first time we met and you won't let me have any silk or paint my dreams, and I think you're trying to hurt me."

"Oh, Paul, that's not so!" said Ben. "Just step out here and we'll talk this over."

"Didn't the sheriff try to burn down my place?"

"Oh, no, Paul, no! Listen, we *need* a painter. I'll get you a gold medal to wear that says 'Town Painter' on it."

"And I could paint my dreams?" Paul asked. He was beginning to believe Ben, who, like a snake, had a way of getting up close and confidential before he struck.

"Dreams, memories, visions, miracles . . . anything," said Ben. "Take my word for it."

Paul laid his brush down and took a step toward the door. "And you'll let me have some silk to paint on?"

"Of course, Paul. Silk or satin or velvet or anything."

Paul hesitated. "I still don't know if I believe you, Mr. Gizzard."

"Listen, Paul," said Ben. "Look here." He stooped and slid off one fancy boot, then the other, and unbuckled the great silver buckle on his trousers. "Paul, you can have all the silk you want, and I'll give you some to start on right now. I just want to show you my heart's in the right place." And he dropped his trousers.

Ben was wearing light blue silk shorts with just the faintest yellow line in them and a delicate pattern of pale pink flowers. Paul stepped to the very entrance of the door to look at this wonder of the undergarment trade. He was one step away from the place where the boulder would come crashing down.

"Just take one more step out here, Paul," said Ben, "and I'll strip these silk shorts off and hand them right to you." He stepped out of his trousers and kicked them aside. Mayor Ben Gizzard stood there in his bare legs, smiling, and innocent Paul, finally fooled, took the step out the door. Ben Gizzard looked up. He nodded, and the boulder rolled off the cliff and fell.

Ben thought he had it perfectly calculated. He stood still, smiling friendly at Paul to hold him in place, thumbs hooked in the top of his shorts as if he was ready to peel them off. The boulder fell, and Ben had calculated wrong. The great rock hit neither of them, but fell just three feet from Ben, landing on the opposite end of the step he was standing on. Ben was shot up into the air like a missile out of a catapult. The air rushed past him and the shack grew small below him. Ben was shaken and surprised, but he knew he would land safely, probably in a water trough or a basket of washing, so he wasn't too worried.

At the very top of the arc, far above Depression Gulch, Ben hung motionless in the air for a deep and silent moment, turning slowly before he started down again. And in that moment, feet pointed into the sky, he saw in the distance, upside down, an enormous snow-covered mountain. Then just for a wink the mountain was blocked out by the dark shape of Paul's black bird, which flew past with its head turned toward Ben. And considering that Ben had been so mean to Paul, the bird gave him a nice compliment.

"Howdy there, Mayor!" it said. "Them's mighty smart-looking shorts you got on."

Then Ben Gizzard began falling.

THE DARK
PRINCESS

To speak no evil is possible for a while, and to hear no evil often means walking away. But to see no evil is most difficult. And if thine eye offend thee, pluck it out. The eyes are also gateways to the soul. Also, we but see through a glass, darkly. And so forth. This is what came of musing on sight and beauty, fools and love.

THERE was a child born who was so beautiful that no one could look at her without blinking, and she was a Princess. Each day and each year she became more beautiful. When she was ten, those who spoke to her looked over her shoulder, or turned their heads while speaking. It was as if a great light shone out of her face. When she was a young lady and ready to marry, no one could look into her face at all. The sight would strike them blind. And another thing. The Princess herself was totally blind.

She was not born blind, but became blind year by year as she became more beautiful. The Royal Physician explained the matter to her parents, the King and Queen. He said the condition was caused by a "frontal optical reversal of the cognitive processes acting on the stereoscopic image-blending phenomenon which resulted in a transposed focal plane bilaterally projecting her sight into a dark area of her brain." He could put it more simply than this. "It is like a dark cloud that blocks out the sun. It could pass at any time."

And so, since it could pass at any time, the King and

Queen kept her blindness a secret. That was easy enough to do, since it was impossible for anyone to look at the Princess directly, and a great, long-haired dog led her way and guarded her step, and she had the measure of every chair and table in the palace, and every bush and tree in the Royal Garden. Her ear was so clever that she knew the footstep of everyone on tile or on carpet, and their voices, of course. From the rustle of their clothes, she knew what others were wearing, and from the tinkle of metal and the clink of stone, their ornaments and jewelry, and no one could sit so quietly in a room that she would not know he was there.

One day, when the Princess was walking in the garden, the King made a wonderful discovery. He was standing at a stained glass window inside the palace as she passed, and his discovery was that he could look into her face through the dark glass and not be blinded. He called her and spoke to her face to face through the window and was awed by her beauty.

Everyone in the Kingdom who could afford it got himself a piece of colored glass to behold the Princess, and watched her come and go with her dog, her head held in a slight attentive cock, as if she were listening to music they could not hear, or pursuing some fancy in her mind. She carried herself with such aloofness that some thought she was conceited about her great beauty and could not bother to take notice of anyone else. Some said it was only modesty and a sign of good upbringing. But it was neither. She was merely counting her steps and listening to the many sounds that tell the way in total darkness, and feeling the trembling of the leash she held as the dog informed her of a chair or table out of place, a new-dug hole in the garden, a limb across a path, or anything else amiss or strange in her way. The people did not suspect she was blind.

Now this was the state of affairs when the first Prince came to the Kingdom to consider the girl for a bride, and through his glass—yes, even so darkly—she was as beautiful to him as anyone he had ever seen, and he loved her at once. After a while of courtly good manners, they walked in the garden alone, led by the Princess's dog. They stopped by a flowering bush, and the Prince looked at her through his glass and spoke.

"Forgive me," he said, "but this past hour has been an age to me, and there would be nothing left of me but dust if I would wait through a season of wooing to declare myself to you. Let me be plain and quick while I am not yet faded to a shadow by the sight of you. You are more beautiful than anyone I have ever seen or could imagine, and I am helplessly in love with you already."

"Are you?" said the Princess, touching a blossom.

"Forsooth," said the Prince, "my very self with love has leaped from me. I have forgotten who I am, in love. I would not know my face in a mirror. Marry me. Come with me and be my Queen, or say no to me and tell me my name so I may despair over the sound of it forever."

The Princess had been told that the Prince was handsome and well set up, and she had no reason to doubt it. His speech was fair (though a bit extravagant), his manners pleasant, and his voice sounded sweet to her.

"If you love me," said the Princess, "then you may prove it to me."

The Prince dropped to one knee. "Only tell me how," he said. "Any vow, any venture, any danger, any dare . . . "

"Look at me," said the Princess.

"What?"

"Take away your piece of colored glass and look at me directly."

"But . . . but . . ." the Prince stammered, getting to his feet again. "They say that, that if one does . . ."

"Yes," said the Princess, "if you do, you will be blinded."

"But to be *blind!*" said the Prince. "How awful. Certainly you wouldn't want me to be blind! Sight is more valuable than anything but life itself. How could you love me then?"

"Only then *could* I love you. Then I would believe that you truly loved me, and I would love you."

The Prince protested such an outrageous test of his love, and drew upon arguments from philosophy, law, physics, chemistry, and astronomy to declare the reasons why he could not meet the test. "Give me another test," he demanded.

"There is no other," said the Princess, and plucking a blossom she turned and walked back to the palace.

The Prince rode away that same day, and the King came to the Princess in her rooms and said, "Did the Prince not please you?"

"He pleased me well enough," she said, brushing the dog with long sweeping strokes, "and I might have loved him,"

"But then why did he leave?" asked the King.

"Because he could not love *me*, Father."

"Ye gods, he must have been blind! Excuse me, dear."

"No, he was not blind," said the Princess. "He would have hated that."

And so for a year the princes came, and each in his manner, shy or bold, plain or poetic, declared he had lost his heart in love for the Princess. But none would lose his sight for it, and all of them went away in a silent and puzzled wonder.

Likewise were the King and Queen puzzled. Princes were now coming from very far away, and soon there would be none left at all to come. They wondered—had the princes suspected that the girl was blind? The King and Queen had chosen to keep this a secret, and did not consider it so very unfair since the girl was likely to regain her sight at any moment. And besides, her blindness was a small thing in comparison to her beauty. They simply could not understand. Of course, they did not know of the test the girl proposed. And none could pass that test.

The Princess by this time had satisfied herself that she would not marry, and in these later days she became sad. It was not so much that she was sad because she would not have a husband, for those who do not marry can be happy, but her sadness was in her doubt that there was such a thing as love in the world. So many had told her that they loved her, but none of them would prove it in the way she asked. Then what was this love they spoke about? She was tired of the word.

The Princess walked more slowly than usual now, and sometimes she sat by a window for hours without moving, and she took no delight in stories or music, and if dessert had not been served after supper, she would not have noticed. It is a bad sadness to believe that there is no love in the world, and people have hanged themselves for less gloomy discoveries.

But it was worse yet than that. Believing that there was no love in the world was her lesser sorrow. Her greater sorrow was this: What if a Prince *should* give up his eyesight out of love for her? What had she to give in return? She was already blind. Just one time there was a Prince who had paused thoughtfully when she told him the test, and for a terrible few throbbing moments she feared that this one would actually go blind for her, and a strange agony rose in her breast, and she was relieved when the Prince began his protest.

Later and alone, the poor girl concluded that her fear and agony in those moments was for the reason that even though there may be love in the world, there was no love in herself. She had nothing to give to prove it. That was her greater sorrow. She believed she could not love.

When her thoughts followed along these dismal lines for too long a time, and she found herself wondering how it would feel to fall from the great tower, and how long it would take before she was broken on the ground, the Princess shook her head and hurried to the kitchen to have a picnic packed for herself, and she took herself away from her thoughts of oblivion, out through the garden and beyond the great stone lion gates on the path that went down to the ocean. Her dog led the way, and as the surf grew louder in the distance and the first smell of salt air came to her, she hummed a tune to raise her spirits. Only the sea was large enough to fill the emptiness she sometimes felt inside herself, and there at the edge of the land where a cliff dropped into the crashing surf below, she would eat her picnic lunch and drink a glass of wine, and sometimes she would smile.

On this day there was someone else out on a picnic at that place. The Court Fool was sitting with his legs dangling over the side of the cliff, and next to him was a bottle of wine and some chicken bones. The dog barked, and the Fool turned to look. He blinked, and quickly got out his piece of colored glass and watched the Princess approach. As usual, she seemed to take no notice of him at all, and it was not his place to greet her first. What a strange, distracted girl she seemed to be, and he concluded that she was probably caught up in a daydream. In fact, she came walking out onto the cliff so purposefully and yet so much like a sleepwalker, that he was certain she was going to walk right over the edge, and he called, "Look out!"

Hardly were the words out of his mouth when she stopped.

"Look out?" she said, turning toward him but looking over his head. "Look out for what? I am exactly five steps from the edge of the cliff." She had recognized his voice, of course. "What are you doing out here, Fool?"

"Well, as you see, Princess, I came for a little picnic like yourself. Roast chicken, a little wine. Will the dog eat the bones?"

"You are certainly a fool if you don't know that chicken bones are dangerous for dogs," she said, and she spread out a cloth to set her picnic basket on. The Fool raked the bones over the side and watched them fall into the surf below. He looked at the Princess again through his colored glass, then took a drink of his wine. He had never been so close to her before, and certainly he had never been alone with her. What could he say? He ventured a common subject: "They say another Prince is coming to visit next week, from very far away."

"I have heard that," said the Princess, breaking some bread and putting a piece of cheese in her mouth. "It matters little."

The Fool had intended to follow up on such a conversation, for he was safe and in his place to talk of the visiting princes, their fine dress and horses, and to gossip of neighboring kingdoms, but instead he said, "Why don't you ever laugh at me?"

The Princess stopped chewing. She started to make a stern face at the Fool, but then she shrugged. "I do laugh, now and again." The truth was, of course, that she had never been able to see his funny antics when he entertained at court, and remembered to laugh only sometimes, when the others laughed.

"No you don't laugh, not really," said the Fool, "and I am a student of laughing. No, you don't laugh, not like the others. And the others laugh when I see them about the hallways and do a face and a little step for them, but you seem to ignore me."

The Princess folded some ham into her bread. "Perhaps you are not such a funny fool as you think you are."

The Fool plucked at the grass and sprinkled it into the

wind blowing up past his legs. "I would think my face was funny enough," he said, and they sat and listened to the ocean. "But I *can* make you laugh," said the Fool at last. "Yes, I could make you laugh this very moment if I wanted to."

"I guarantee you cannot," said the Princess, and she smiled. "Stand on your head, stretch out your cheeks and ears, look at me under your legs, and squash your nose. You couldn't make me laugh."

"Then I will, just to show you," said the Fool. "And I will do it with words alone. Be ready to laugh, now, for here it is that will amuse you greatly, and only three words will do it." He took a double gulp of wine and then said, "I love you."

The Princess did not laugh. She lowered her head and gazed very solemnly toward the ground. Presently she said, "Yes, for a Fool to love a Princess—I suppose that might be funny. However, since it isn't true, it isn't funny. Two-score princes have come and gone, and all of them said that they loved me. But none of them did, and you do not, either."

The Princess poured herself a glass of wine and took a sip. "There is no such thing as love, and that's why I don't laugh at you now, and why I rarely laugh. What you think you love you do not, really. I am only beautiful, and if you lost the way to see me, you would not love me."

"No," he said. "It is not your beauty I love, it is *you* I love, it is your *ways* I love. A Fool may look closely to know who a person is, and with little insult, for he need only wag his nose to be excused. And though I have seen you only darkly, I have seen you deeply, and it is you yourself that I love."

Now the Princess did laugh. "Let me tell you something. Will you promise to keep it a secret?"

"In my heart," said the Fool. And so the Princess told him why she had not chosen a Prince to marry, and how she had put her test to them, and how they all had declined to look at her directly and go blind for their love.

"I would be blind for you," said the Fool.

The Princess gathered up her things and put them in the basket. "Then you would be a fool for sure." She folded her picnic cloth and stood up. "Yes, you would be the best fool of all. Any of the princes would have had me for a bride upon looking at me directly. But I cannot marry you, and you would have nothing for it but darkness."

The Fool smiled to himself and nodded. Then he too stood up next to her and looked at her through his colored glass. The Princess could feel the Fool's sadness, and she spoke again before turning to leave.

"You are a good and fortunate fool to believe in love, but your sadness is not as great as it could be. Mine is greater. Remember, I do not believe in love."

"But you *must* believe in love," said the Fool. "I would go blind that you do, for that alone I would go blind."

And then the Princess was reminded of her greater sorrow—her sorrow that even though another might one day give his sight out of love for her, she had nothing to give in return. She shook her head.

"Ah, dear Fool, we could be certain of nothing except

that you would be blind. How could I believe? I have nothing to give in return. But here, let me touch your hand before I go."

The Princess reached out her hand, and she felt a thin, smooth object placed in her palm. She caught her breath to cry out, but the Fool cried, "Oh, oh . . . " and she heard him stumble backwards, and heard his foot slide on the cliff's edge. He fell without a sound, and she heard him splash in the surf below. She dropped the picnic basket and the piece of colored glass, touched her toe to the edge of the cliff, and leaped into the water to save him, for he was only newly blind.

And there in the darkness below they touched for a moment, and then they drowned.

And in that moment they touched, the sun rose a million times for them, and the Princess and the Fool could see each other and all the things of life and the world more clearly than but a dozen people since the beginning of time. And that moment they touched outlasted the life of the King and Queen, and outlasted the life of the Kingdom. And that moment they touched is lasting still, and will outlast us, too.

STINKY PETE

This poem was published in a book called Delta Baby & 2 Sea Songs, *wherein also was published "The Wreck of the Linda Dear." The title poem, "Delta Baby," carried on rather too much, but began:*

> Delta baby cry and scream,
> Lay upon your boat and dream.

We can forget the rest of it. This came off the television, and I only half heard it. "What did he say?" I asked my wife. "Did he say delta baby cry and scream?" Actually, the man was talking about the Vietnam War.

THERE SAILED a pirate called Stinky Pete,
a black-hearted villain with dirty feet,
whose crew was scum from head to toe.
His first mate's name was Snotty-nose Joe.

They cut a path on the open sea,
sliced out gizzards and heard no plea
for mercy, fairness, or "In God's name!"
And dogfights next to them were tame.

So one brisk morning while out for spoil,
they spied a ship rigged up all royal,
and fancy dandies strolled the deck,
with lacy collars around their necks.

"Avast!" cried Pete. "The Lord bless me,
them fops is all dressed out for tea.
Stick 'em through their buttonholes—
I wouldn't cut up such fine clothes."

The scurvy crew came round to port,
slobbering curses and came athwart
the goodly ship and swung aboard,
their cruddy teeth clamped on their swords.

The men they fought were clean and shaven,
with courage to fight and not one craven,
but at close quarters they gave up trying.
The pirates' smell was worse than dying.

They all then soon gave up the fray,
dropped their swords and started to pray,
and holding their noses they all withdrew,
to the upwind side of the pirate crew.

"Run out the plank!" yelled Stinky Pete.
"The sharks are waiting for their treat."
And Snotty-nose Joe got the men all tied,
for their last short walk on over the side.

He ran his nose down his sleeve and said,
"All set, Captain," and he tore a shred
of cloth from his shirt and covered the eyes
of the first of the men that was doomed to die.

He was lifted up and set on the plank,
while cutlasses poked him about the flanks,
and the scummy pirates laughed at the fun.
Stinky Pete chuckled and scratched at his bum.

Then just as the man teetered on the verge,
from out of the cabin a girl emerged.
"You there!" she cried. "You rank rapscallion!
Are you the captain of that filthy galleon?"

It was Princess Ann, out sailing for pleasure,
and she marched up to Pete and took his measure.
Said she to Pete, "You smell like a reef,
and don't you ever brush your teeth?"

"Belay that!" roared Pete. "Or I'll haul your keel!"
But she grabbed his nose and made him kneel,
and called to her Ladies, who were waiting aside,
for some soap and water to scrub Pete's hide.

They got out tubs, and soaps and lotions,
and dunked the pirates in the ocean,
and scoured them all till they turned bright pink,
then sent them to wash their clothes in a sink.

"Just powder yourselves while you're there," said Ann.
They meekly turned and said, "Yes ma'am."
"Tend your nails and trim your beards,
brush your teeth and clean out your ears."

Snotty-nose Joe she took by the hair,
and from a petticoat had him tear
ten squares of cloth. "Now use a hanky
to blow your nose!" And Joe said, "Thank 'ee."

She lined them up in an hour or so,
at the poop deck rail and made them show
their ears and nails, and then she charged,
"Get over and clean up your filthy barge."

Two days working those pirates ran,
under the eye of Princess Ann.
They mopped and brushed and shined their ship,
then Ann inspected, and found it fit.

"Farewell," she called, as they drifted apart.
"You're clean outside, now clean your hearts.
If ever again you pirate this sea,
I'll catch you sure, and you'll answer to me."

So off they sailed, and Snotty-nose Joe
is now called Sniffles, and always blows.
Stinky is now called Soapy Pete,
smells of lavender, and has clean feet.

And ever since their run-in with Ann,
they've not been pirates with bloody hands,
but they trade in silks, and spices and tea,
and they're nice and sweet as sailors *can* be.

CRAZY IN LOVE

The story was originally about vanity, and my first image of it was of a woman in a shed pushing around a great revolving mirror in a domed and jewelled minaret set on the ground, and some crazy things were to happen. But then I thought, if I make it a plain rustic shed, and make a young man and woman in love, then nothing need be crazy at all, except for that, which is sufficient.

THERE WAS a young woman who lived alone on a small farm far in the country. She worked alone, and ate alone, and sighed alone, and slept alone, and cried alone. And when she laughed, which was not often, she laughed alone. Her name was Diana.

Now one beautiful spring day she was working in the garden. With her head down, she chopped at the earth with her hoe. The sweet breeze blew her long hair across her face. Several times she brushed it back over her shoulders, but at last she threw down the hoe and said aloud, "Oh, this is impossible!"

The work was not that hard, but the spring breeze and the singing of the woodland birds and the gentle warmth of the sun were difficult to bear. She wanted to turn to someone and say "Here, see!" and "There, listen!" and "Touch this!" And she wanted just to look at someone and share the spring day. She was young, and she was tired of being alone. Arching her back in a stretch, she looked down the narrow roadway that passed her place. But rarely did anyone come down that roadway. Rarely did Diana go up that roadway to town. There were goats to milk every twelve hours. Sighing deeply, she gave the hoe a feeble kick.

Diana reached in her pocket then for a piece of string, and she was tying back her hair when she heard a birdcall that pleased her especially. She walked out of the garden toward the sound and into the woods. When the bird called again, she followed the sound. "Not a phoebe," she said to herself. "No, and not a vireo." She stepped lightly now, hoping to catch a glimpse of the bird. It called again, and she followed. "Nor a hermit thrush, either," she mused, and she followed.

In a short while, Diana found herself in a part of the woods that was strange to her. She had not spied the bird she sought, which now had stopped singing. "Ah, too bad," she said, and turned back on her way. But then she heard a singing again. Only this time it was not the song of a bird. It was a woman's voice, farther off in those unknown woods. But no one lives over that way, Diana thought to herself. The brush was thicker there, and she had to part it with a stick as she moved toward the voice, which continued singing. The more clearly she heard it, the sweeter it was; but the song was a slow and sad song, nearly like a wail or a lament.

In another few minutes Diana parted her way through some heavy bushes, and at once she was standing on the edge of a small glade which was nearly in the shape of a circle. Wild flowers were dotted about the edges of the glade, and the grass within looked almost cared for by a gardener, so nicely was it cropped by deer. A fresh breeze blew across the small meadow, and several birds sang in the near woods. And there, in the middle of the glade, bathed in the gentle sunshine, was an old broken-down shack. From out of the shack, very distinctly now, came the voice of a woman, high and sad and lonely, singing her song.

Diana walked across the grass, slightly bent forward and hesitant, for she had a notion she might be trespassing. She walked right up to the shack. Some boards were loose. Diana set her feet carefully and peered between two of the boards to see who the strange singer was in this peculiar place. Immediately as she looked in, she raised her hand to her mouth to silence her gasp of astonishment and distress. For there in the little shack was a beautiful woman in a white robe who was chained to a great millstone. She was singing her sad song as she pushed the great stone around and around.

Diana could not keep her voice in. "Oh!" she cried, and leaped to the door of the shack, pushed it open and ran to the beautiful chained woman. "Oh," Diana cried again, "who has done this to you? What cruelty has been done here, what monster has chained you to this stone? Oh, let me break these chains, let me find a tool to set you free." And she began searching the small shack for a piece of iron to break the chains. The beautiful woman stopped pushing the millstone. She looked with tenderness and sympathy upon Diana. Then she spoke.

"Nay, do not rush about so, for you cannot release me from these chains. This is no cruelty, and no monster has imprisoned me here. This that I do, and that I am here, is an enchantment, and only a certain passing of time can set me free. Come, talk to me as I go around."

Diana was not much calmed by this gentle and patient answer. She came to the beautiful woman and covered her hands with her own, and helped her push. "Oh, dear!" said Diana. "This is terrible! Surely something can be done."

"Nothing for me this moment," said the woman. "But I can do something for you. I can grant your wish."

"My wish? I have no wish but to set you free."

"You must think," said the woman, "for there is another wish you have. I know this, because no one may find me here except that they have a wish very dear to them. No one may hear my song unless they have a deep longing. So think carefully now. What is it you wish for?"

Diana walked around slowly with the chained woman, and she remembered that surely she did have a wish most close to her heart. And she blushed.

"Ah," said the beautiful woman, noticing.

"All right, then," said Diana, throwing her head back. "Don't you know? I wish I had a husband, and that he loved me and that I loved him, and that we could share our lives together."

"Then you shall have a husband," said the woman. "Your wish is granted. But you must do something for me in return."

"Oh, I will very gladly, and for nothing except to make this hard task easier for you."

"I know that, my dear, but nevertheless you shall have a husband, and this is what I ask in return." The beautiful woman then bent her head toward her closely chained hands and said, "There, you see? I haven't even the freedom to brush my hair with my fingers. Day after day with the dust and the sweat and the falling about my shoulders it has become terribly tangled and stringy and knotted. Once it was beautiful, and I hate that I cannot care for it properly."

Diana immediately put her hands up and began unsnarling the chained woman's long hair.

"Thank you, dear, but you must bring a brush, and you must walk around with me and brush my hair and talk with me, for I am lonesome. Will you do this to get a husband?"

"I would do it anyway."

"But when you have a husband, then you *must* do it. That must be your promise. Every day you must come here alone to walk with me for one hour and brush my hair, to be a comfort and company to me. That is what I ask."

"That is no hard promise," said Diana, "and I promise it with gladness."

The woman smiled and spoke for the last time. "Leave now. And when you have a husband, remember me. Take your hairbrush from home and come to me. This is your promise. Now, farewell."

Immediately the beautiful woman began singing again. Diana walked to the door of the shack, said "Farewell," and strode out across the glade, into the forest, and home.

Now all this happened early in the day, and Diana was making a fire for the midday meal when she heard a call from outside the house.

"Hey! Cut and stack some wood for a dinner?"

She looked out the window. There stood a young man, a woodcutter, with a bucksaw over his shoulder and an axe in his hand.

"You could split some wood!" she yelled back at him. "Right there!" She pointed to a pile of wood.

The young man twirled the saw off his shoulder, spit on his hands, and walked up to the splitting block with a professional eye on the stack of wood. "I can do that little bit before you can boil a potato." He smiled at Diana, kicked a round of wood from the stack, set it on the splitting block, and turning to Diana again said, "Ready . . . Go!" Then he slung into his work. Diana opened her mouth, closed it, and ran to get a potato.

They also had a salad, warmed-up roast chicken, some peach preserves, and at last were enjoying their coffee. The young man took out his pipe and said, "Do you mind?" Diana shook her head. He filled the pipe with tobacco and punched it down with his thumb. Then lit up. He glanced around, then stuck the burned match behind his ear. So, sitting comfortably at the table by the window that looked toward the woods, they talked.

It was Diana who talked mostly, and although she was a bit past her good manners for the many questions she asked, it could be understood. She had so little company. The woodcutter himself seemed not to mind, and he answered openly and in good humor.

"Then you have no home?" Diana asked for the second time.

"Only where I lay my back at night," said the young man. He took a deep puff at his pipe. "But it's a good life.

I go where I wish. I have my axe and my saw, I have my work. That's home to me." He studied his pipe and then added, as if woodcutting were a highly appointed office: "But that sort of life isn't for everyone of course. There's many couldn't do it."

Diana nodded and waited for him to go on.

"Oh, yes, there's hardship sometimes. There's a lot to say for carrying your home around with you and eating on the way, only you've got to be lucky sometimes or you *don't* eat. Here's an example right now. I was lucky your man wasn't here when I happened by, or else he'd not let me split that wood for dinner and I'd have to go on and be hungry."

"That wasn't lucky," said Diana. "I just have no man."

The young man looked at his pipe again, and cleared his throat. He looked up. "Ah . . . my name is Dan," he said.

"My name is Diana."

They both looked down. Dan started to tap the bowl of his pipe on his boot. He glanced up. Diana nodded.

"You know," he said, knocking the pipe and sticking it back in his pocket, "that was a fine dinner. I don't know when I've had such a good dinner lately."

"But I didn't even reckon on having a guest."

"That don't matter about how good it was," said Dan.

"The chicken was a bit dry, being leftovers."

"I hardly noticed."

"Just barely," said Diana. "I just barely noticed."

"In fact," said Dan, "I didn't notice at all."

"Well," said Diana, "neither did I."

They smiled at each other, then for a moment were

silent. Dan tapped a finger on the table and looked around the floor.

"I admire the way you stacked that wood," Diana said.

"You do?"

"Sometimes it falls over when I stack it."

"Well, I was hungry, you know, and hurrying a little, but I can stack it better than that. You noticed how that west corner is a little crooked?"

"I just hardly noticed at all."

"Not much, just barely. I barely noticed it myself."

"In fact," said Diana, "I didn't notice it at all."

"Come to think of it," said Dan, "neither did I."

Again they smiled, and again they fell silent. Dan jumped in his seat when Diana spoke to him next.

"What are you looking around the floor for?"

"Ma'am," said Dan. "I mean Diana. I'd sure like to do some more work for you instead of going right on down the road. I could split and stack enough wood for a week before suppertime, if you'd be kind enough to share your table with me again."

Diana closed her eyes and touched her lips with her fingers thoughtfully. "That shoat pig is ready for butchering," she said, and opened her eyes and looked brightly at him. "Have you ever ate roast suckling pig with cranberry glaze?"

"Ohhhh, ma'am," Dan said, slapping his belly with both hands and pushing his chair back. "I mean Diana. I just got to get at that wood."

So they both went about their work, and whenever he came up with wood from the forest, she was near the window and would wave out at him. And he would wave back and sometimes let out a yell and go galloping off into the woods again like a clown; and she laughed, and he turned and laughed back.

The day passed wonderfully for both in their work. The wood, enough for a week, was stacked beautifully, and the roast suckling pig with cranberry glaze was delicious. And any two people would have said so, even if they weren't falling in love. Dan lit his pipe over coffee when they had finished with the strawberry shortcake, and she pushed the lid of a jar toward him. He dropped the match in it and smiled, then let out a sigh.

"Tired?" Diana asked.

"Tired? No." He drew on his pipe. "Just thinking."

"Just thinking?" she said.

"About wood," said Dan.

"About wood?"

"About how I spend most of my day cutting wood for people, and how I never really get to see the best part of it."

"How do you mean that?"

"I mean when I leave. I mean when I go along the road and it's getting dark, or when I'm sleeping in a field, and I watch the smoke come out of a chimney, and the little sparks. I know it's wood I cut there in the fireplace that's doing it, and the people are sitting around and talking, or maybe just being quiet and watching into the fire, being together." Dan took a puff on his pipe. "But I never get to see that part of it. I don't have any times like that."

"It is beautiful," said Diana. "But if you're alone you

don't often do that either, just sit by the fire and watch. It's something that almost needs two people to enjoy for as much as it's worth."

"That's my thinking," said Dan.

There wasn't anything more said for a long while, and a slight chill came into the house as the stove fire burned down. They found themselves staring into the dark fireplace, and in the same moment looked at each other.

"I could start a fire in the fireplace," Diana said quietly.

And just as quietly, Dan said, "I could get some good heartwood from outside."

So in a short while they were sitting before a fine fire, and they talked together and dreamed at it until it was late and time for bed. Dan said he'd be much obliged to sleep in the barn, but Diana said he could sleep on the floor, and she doubled up the rug for a mattress and brought him a quilt. She knelt on the floor to smooth out his bedding. He knelt across from her and helped. His hands touched hers. Then they were holding hands and looking at each other. And then they were kissing.

The smell of bacon and eggs woke Dan. He jammed his legs into his trousers, looped into his suspenders, and clomped to the kitchen table in his untied boots. Diana turned from the stove and watched him tie his boots.

"Coffee?" Diana said.

"Lovely," Dan said.

They ate breakfast one-handed, for they were holding hands with the other, except when they buttered the toast.

Dan finished and said, "You are the best cook in the whole world."

"And you're the best woodcutter," Diana said.

"Yesterday was nothing," Dan said. "Yesterday I was only *half* alive. You watch me cut wood today." He stood up.

"Not right now," Diana said. "Later. Right now let's go to town and get married."

Dan took her hand. She stood up and he put his arms around her waist, and she, her arms around his neck. "Right now let's do that," said Dan. And they kissed awhile, tasting like bacon and eggs and buttered toast and other good things.

And they did that. They went to town and got married. They walked all about the town after that, looking at the houses and the bridges and the churches and the people working and in shops. Then they listened to a small street band and watched a goat who appeared to be dancing. Very often they laughed, and less often they were so quiet and serious and so far away in their eyes that you might have thought they'd never find their way back. But a child playing across their path or a chasing dog would bring them back with a laugh. Everyone could see that they were in love.

They stayed that night in a small inn. The innkeeper's and his wife's eyes twinkled at them. The wife said to them that it was a nice room, and the innkeeper said it was a nice bed. After they had left, Diana stared out of the window, while Dan stared at a picture on the wall. Neither of them had the slightest idea what they were seeing. Then Dan and Diana went to bed on their wedding night.

*   *   *

Now the next day, when they had returned to their small place in the country, they had just finished the midday dinner when Diana got up and took her hairbrush from the dresser.

"I think I'll go for a walk in the woods," she said.

She remembered her promise to the chained lady with the tangled hair. She would go out now and brush her hair and walk with her for an hour, and talk with her, to keep her promise, because her wish for a husband had been granted.

"Good," said Dan. "I'll finish this pipe and we'll go together."

"No, dear, I believe I'll go alone."

"Oh?" Dan said, and looked at her for a few moments. "Well . . . all right." He watched her go out the door, then watched her from the window as she walked into the woods, hairbrush in hand. "Huh!" he grunted, and got himself another cup of coffee.

Diana found the small fresh glade without much trouble, for again the singing led her. She entered the door with joy and her heart full of talk to share with the beautiful woman. Together they walked around, the chained woman pushing the heavy millstone and Diana unsnarling and brushing her long hair.

"And is he handsome?" asked the lady.

"More handsome than I can tell you, although most people would hardly notice it. And strong, and tender, and who would believe such rough hands could touch so softly?"

"Tell me about the town, then. What did you see, where did you go?"

Diana told everything she could think of, and very shortly, so it seemed to them both, the hour was up and they parted. "Again tomorrow," said the enchanted lady.

"Again tomorrow," said Diana happily. "There is much more to tell you. Oh, it's wonderful."

"Then tomorrow."

"Then," said Diana. She left, and hurried across the glade and into the forest.

When she returned to the house, Dan asked her if she had enjoyed her walk in the woods. She said she had enjoyed it very much, and Dan said, "Hmmmmmm . . ."

Then it was evening. Then it was night. Then it was morning the next day, then the sun was high, and then they ate. After eating, Diana took up her hairbrush and said, "I believe I'll go for a walk in the woods."

"I'll go, too," said Dan, knocking his pipe out on his boot.

"No," Diana said, touching his shoulder. He sat down again. "I'll go alone. I enjoy a walk alone."

"Hmmmm," Dan said. "Well . . ."

She was gone out the door. Dan watched her from the window as she entered the forest. He rubbed his chin and again said, "Hmmmm."

"He is *so* wonderful," Diana said to the chained lady. "And funny, too. Let me tell you what he did last night." So they talked and walked around together. Diana brushed her companion's hair and they smiled and laughed. Near the end of the hour, Diana was quiet for a time. Then she asked, "How did you come to be chained up like this? Because it does seem a cruel thing, this enchantment."

"No, not cruel," said the lady. "Haven't you guessed? This is a punishment, and something I have deserved."

"A punishment? Then for what, dear lady? Oh, I shouldn't ask that. Forgive me."

"Don't be troubled," said the woman. "In time the enchantment will wear off, and I am happy to tell you how it came about, since it is a lesson. You see, I was once one of those people who do not believe in enchantments. And because of that, I must suffer to be enchanted myself, and to be chained and push this millstone around."

"Oh, how unfortunate," said Diana. And she meant how unfortunate that the woman had never believed in enchantments, for Diana never had any doubts about enchantments. "And how long must this be? Not that I regret that I must come and visit with you, but I ask only for your sake. How soon will you be free?"

"There is no knowing that," said the woman. "But one day you will come to me and you won't find me here. That will mean that I am free and that you are free of your promise, and I will never be here again."

This visit ended in silence and sadness. And as Diana entered the forest to go home, she listened to the enchanted lady's lonely singing, and she wept.

"Have you been crying?" Dan asked when she came in.

"Only a very little," Diana said. She smiled at him. "But I am very happy."

Dan could not understand this at all. He felt awkward around his wife that evening. It seemed he could not find the right things to say, and he watched her and wondered what was troubling her.

*   *   *

The next day at the regular time, Diana said that she was going for a walk in the woods.

"Good," Dan said, stuffing his pipe. He didn't look up.

She paused at the door and looked at him over her shoulder. "Wouldn't you want to go with me?" she asked, even though she would not have allowed it.

"No," said Dan. "I'll do a little work in the garden."

"Hmmmm," she said, and out she went, looking back once more before she entered the forest.

Then Dan was immediately up and out of his chair. He stuck his hat on, watched the woods for a minute, then ran to where his wife had disappeared. He was going to find out where she walked all alone. And he worried about her crying. There was now the very rough beginning of a path where his wife had trod on her errand, and he followed it slowly, careful not to come too close to the sound of his Diana whisking through the brush up ahead of him.

Presently he heard a donkey bray. It was off in the direction he was following. He crouched low, parted the bushes carefully, and he almost stumbled into the glade when he came upon it. But he pulled back behind a bush and looked. There in the center of the small glade was an old shack, and he could hear his wife's voice inside it. She seemed to be talking to someone. Now what could all this be? he wondered. He left the bush on his hands and knees and crawled across the grass until he was right up against the shack and looking through a broken board.

And there inside was his wife, walking around and around with an old donkey that was pushing a millstone, and she was brushing the old donkey's mane and talking to it, telling the animal all about the time of the day past, and about himself.

Dan was stunned. He fell back sitting on the grass. Dragging himself across the glade into the hiding bushes, he crept in and leaned on a tree. "Oh, oh!" he said aloud. "Oh, my poor wife is crazy! My poor wife is completely mad. Oh, I have married a poor crazy wife!"

The thought of it fairly scattered his senses, and he wandered off toward home. "Oh! Each day she goes out and combs a donkey's mane and talks to it like it was a person. How long has this been going on? What can I do?"

Dan had never known a crazy person, and he didn't at all know what was best to do or say, and he was very confused. Therefore he got lost on the way home, but he found a stream that led back. He sat for a while on the bank, resting. He held his head in his hands and rocked and moaned for his poor crazy wife. Then he heard a voice call out to him.

"Hey, youngster, you got any tobacco?"

Dan looked up. There was no one else on the stream bank. The voice called again.

"Over here! You got any tobacco? I sure could use a smoke."

And there! There in the middle of the stream, sitting on a mound of sticks, was an old man with a white beard, dressed in overalls. Dan stared for a moment, then said, "Yeah, I've got some tobacco. What are you doing out there? If you want a smoke, swim on in."

"Can't," said the old man. "I'm enchanted, and I got to

sit out here on these sticks till it wears off. Sure do miss my tobacco. Would you mind swimming out here so an old man could have a smoke?"

"Enchanted?"

"You got it. Enchanted right down to my toes. Now hold that tobacco over your head so it don't get wet, mind."

Dan studied the distance across the water. The stream wasn't swift, and possibly he could wade out to the old man.

"Hold on there, grandfather," he said, then took out his pipe, matches, and tobacco. Carefully, he stepped into the water. It came up to his knees, then to his waist, then up to his chest, but his footing was solid. Only for the last couple of yards did Dan have to paddle with one arm, all the while holding the tobacco safe in the air in his free hand.

"Easy there, son," the old man cautioned. He gripped Dan's arm when he was near enough and pulled him up onto the pile of sticks. And there they sat.

Dan handed the tobacco and pipe to the old man, who made up a smoke while Dan squeezed his wet clothes. He studied the old man while he lit up and took a great draw on the pipe.

"Ahhhhhh . . ." said the old man.

"Did you say *enchanted?*" Dan asked.

"Um." The old man took another draw on the pipe and passed it to Dan. "Yep. Just as soon not talk about it. But that's my problem." He tapped his fingers and looked at the pipe. Dan took a smoke and handed it back. "And what's your problem, son? I seen you sitting over there with a burden on your mind so heavy I almost hated to call out, but you know how it is with smoking if you got the habit.

What's your grief, son?" He smoked and watched Dan.

Dan put his head in his hands again. "It's my wife," he said.

"Uh-huh," said the old man. "Woman trouble. Might have known it. Well, I can give you a wish, if you think maybe that'd help."

"A wish?"

"Sure. Nobody sees me out here unless they need a wish, so I guess you need one. Couple of years ago some fellow was fishing that little falls up there above us. Smoking a pipe, too. Fished all day and smoked all day. It about drove me crazy, that smoke drifting down here. I shouted at him for hours, promised him all sorts of stuff, but he didn't notice at all. See—he didn't need a wish, so he didn't see me or hear me." The old man took a long draw off the pipe and passed it back to Dan. "So what's wrong about your wife? You can make a wish for it to be different. She getting fat, ugly, ornery, skinny?"

"She's . . . crazy."

The old man was silent for a while. Then he said, "If you ain't going to smoke any, pass that pipe back." Dan did. "Crazy, huh? Well, I known some crazy people in my time. What's it like with your wife?"

"Every day," Dan began and he sniffed and wiped his eyes. "Every day, grandfather, she goes off into the woods to an old mill. She goes in there, where there's an old donkey, and she brushes its mane and walks around with it and talks to it like it was a real person."

The old man nodded and spit in the water. "Well, there's worse things can happen with a woman than taking up with a donkey. Might be best just to let it be." The old man let this meditation sink in, then he spoke again. "But if you really want it so she doesn't go off visiting donkeys anymore, you can take a wish on it and that's the way it'll be."

"You can do this? You can give me a wish?"

"Yep, just like I said. You get a wish, and if you like her better not crazy, that's how you'll have her."

"Then I wish it," Dan said.

"Then that's it," said the old man. "But you got to do something for me, you know."

Dan nodded eagerly. "Anything, grandfather."

"Each day you got to come out here and smoke with me, and keep me company for about an hour. That all right with you?"

"And then my wife won't be crazy anymore?"

"In a little while. You got to watch for it. Generally shows up in the eyes. You'll know when she's all right. And when she is, then you don't have to come out here anymore." The old man took one last long draw at the pipe and gave it back to Dan. "You go now, and I'll see you tomorrow."

"But can I believe you?" Dan said. "I mean, this talk about enchantments and wishes . . ."

The old man sighed and looked up and down the stream. "I'd advise you to believe it," he said. "Go on now." He pushed Dan off his seat. "Just remember to come back tomorrow about this time. Your wife will be all right."

Dan entered the water with pipe, matches and tobacco held over his head. When he reached the shore he turned and waved.

"Just don't forget the tobacco," said the old man.

Dan followed the stream and found his way home by an easy route, which he would remember for the next day's visit with the old man. Diana was already in the house when he arrived.

"How did you get so wet?" she asked.

"Oh . . . I fell in the stream."

"That was careless," she said.

The next day, after finishing the midday dinner, Diana took up her brush and announced that she would go for a walk in the woods. Dan said that was fine, and he poured another cup of coffee.

"Are you feeling all right?" Diana asked him.

"Fine," said Dan, and be settled himself at the table.

She went out. Dan watched her go toward the woods. A couple of times she looked back, and Dan pulled his head out of sight so she would not see him watching her.

A minute after she entered the woods, he stuck his hat on, patted his shirt pocket to make sure he had his pipe and tobacco, then went out the back door and down to the stream. He easily found his way downstream to where the old man was sitting on the pile of sticks, exactly the same as the day before.

"Hey!" yelled the old man. "I been thinking about you all morning. I mean I been thinking about smoking, but you're all right, too. Now don't get that tobacco wet, son."

In a couple of minutes they were sitting together. Dan got the pipe going and passed it to the old man.

"She ain't no better, grandfather."

"Takes time," said the old man, puffing. "But you got your wish. She'll be all right. You'll know when it happens. Then you won't have to come out here anymore."

Dan smoked then. "How long have you been enchanted out here, grandfather?"

"Too long."

"How come you're enchanted?"

"Don't like to talk about it," said the old man.

"Did you do something wrong?"

"Not much, I didn't think." He gazed into the bowl of the pipe. "Well, I'll tell you, son. Time was, a long time ago, I didn't use to believe in enchantments. I used to scoff and make fun of that sort of stuff, you know. Had no use for it. So this is a kind of punishment. Now I got to be enchanted for a bit, till I learn my lesson."

"Ain't you learned it yet?"

"Well, I ain't as skeptical as I used to be, I tell you that much. But tell me about yourself. Tell me about your place. You got goats? What's your main crop?"

So Dan began telling him all about the farm, and what they raised and what they did. They talked about fertilizers, and goats, and rabbits and such until the hour was up. Dan said good-bye then and slid into the water, holding the tobacco over his head.

"See you tomorrow," he called.

"See you tomorrow," the old man answered.

Diana was home when he arrived. She had been wondering why Dan had left a full cup of coffee on the table, as if he had left the house suddenly. When she saw him, she was convinced that something was strange.

"Did you fall in the stream again?" she asked.

"Huh? Oh, yeah . . . fell in the stream again," Dan said.

Diana made no comment on that, but she watched him all that evening and thought that he was acting odd, though she could not quite understand what was different about him. A couple of times she said, "Are you feeling all right, dear?"

"Sure, why not," Dan answered, and he looked at her closely. "And are *you* feeling all right, dear?"

"I'm fine, dear."

"Well, I'm fine, too."

Yet she knew something was wrong somehow.

So the next afternoon after eating, she picked up her hairbrush and told Dan she was going off to the woods. Dan said that was fine, and that he would fool around the place, maybe fix some fence. So she left and went into the woods, and Dan got his tobacco together and went out the back door.

But Diana saw him. She was hiding behind a bush to fool him because she thought something was certainly peculiar, and she was worried. How could a man fall in the stream two days in a row like that, and now what was he doing sneaking off out the back door? Diana meant to find out what the trouble was. Maybe, she thought, he has fits and falls into the water. Maybe, she thought, he is sick and needs help. Maybe he's keeping his fits a secret from me.

She came out from behind the bush when Dan was gone

a ways, and she ran across to where he had walked toward the stream, following his path. It was easy to follow, for it wove right down beside the stream, and presently she could hear his voice in the distance. Carefully, slowly, she crept up near and parted some bushes to look.

And there in the middle of the stream on a pile of sticks was her husband, dripping wet, sitting next to an old gray beaver, smoking his pipe and calling the beaver "grandfather" and talking about farming.

Diana clapped both hands to her mouth. She scuttled and crawled through the bush for several yards before she dared to let her breath out in a gasp and a wail as she moved farther off from the stream.

"Ohhhhhh . . . ohhhhhhhh, my husband is crazy. Oh, oh, I have married a crazy man, a poor crazy man. Oh, oh, what am I to do?" She curled up by a tree and moaned and held her head. "Oh, my poor crazy husband, oh, oh." Finally she remembered the chained lady and at once was hopeful. "She'll know what to do about this! Surely she'll know something to do. Maybe I can get a wish to make him well again. Quick, now, which is the way?"

And she did find the way after a bit. She broke through the bushes into the glade and ran to the little mill and swung open the door. But there inside was only an old donkey pushing around a millstone. The enchantment was over. The chained lady was free, just as she had said she'd be one day, and Diana would never find her at the mill again. There was nothing left to do but sit down and cry for poor crazy Dan. Then she went home.

*   *   *

When Dan arrived home that afternoon, Diana was in bed. Her worry was working on her health. Dan could see she had been crying.

"I was only thinking about some things," she said to Dan. "I'm well enough." She brought his face down and kissed him. "But are you all right, dear?"

"I fell in the stream again."

"That's all right," she said, stroking his hair. "It doesn't matter."

Dan was puzzled. Now and then when she looked at him that evening, her eyes would brim up with tears. Dan wondered if that meant she was more crazy or less crazy. It seemed maybe more crazy to him, and he began doubting that his wish was helping her any. So they both worried a lot that evening, and they couldn't find much to say. And they sort of tiptoed around and kept offering to get something or do something for each other. That night they held each other tight, and each could feel the other's tears, but they said nothing.

The next morning passed quietly also. She worried about his craziness and how he had cried that night, and he worried about her craziness and her crying. They watched each other, and each thought that the other's watching was more craziness.

When they finished the midday meal, Dan sat dumbly and forgot to light his pipe. He waited for Diana to get her hairbrush and head on out to the woods. He was sad to think that his poor wife was going out to brush a donkey's mane and talk to it. But Diana would go out there no more.

The chained lady was free, gone forever. Presently Dan spoke, for he was eager to talk with the old man again and tell him that his wife was getting worse.

"Aren't you going for a walk in the woods, dear?"

"No, I think not," Diana said.

"Oh. Later then, I suppose."

"No. Not later, either."

"Tomorrow, then?" asked Dan.

"Not tomorrow, either," said Diana.

Dan came up in his chair and looked closely at her, a slight hope rising in him. "But don't you want to take your hairbrush out to the woods and do something?"

"No," she said. "But of course if *you* want to go for a walk, we could go together."

And then Dan saw in his wife's eyes that she was not crazy anymore, just as the old man said it would be. Diana spoke again.

"But I suppose you'll want to go for a walk by yourself, won't you? I mean maybe you'll want to go down by the stream and have a smoke or something?"

"Not me," said Dan, because now his wish was granted. And now there was no reason to go smoke and talk with the old man. "I guess I'll just stay around here."

"But tomorrow you'll go, won't you?"

"No, not tomorrow either. Why don't we just go for a walk together?"

And then Diana saw that *he* wasn't crazy anymore. They smiled at each other, each in a joy unknown to the other, ready to laugh or cry with relief and happiness. But just at that moment, before they could do either, a little man about five inches tall came flying up to the open window, flapping his arms like mad. There was a great earthworm slung over his shoulder, and he lit on a tree branch outside the window. For a moment he panted from the exertion of flying, then shouted in at them.

"Hey, in there! Look at me! I'm a little enchanted man. I've got to live like a bird and eat the things birds eat, and I hate it. It's a punishment. Well, never mind that. But you see this worm I caught? They taste terrible raw, but they ain't so bad cooked up a little. If you'll pop it into the oven for a bit and then toss it out here, I'll give you both a wish."

Dan and Diana looked out, but they did not see the little man, for they did not need a wish. They had everything they needed, everything they could wish for. All they saw was a robin sitting on the branch. All they could hear was chirping.

"My," said Diana. "listen to how excited he is."

"Almost like he's talking to us," Dan said.

"Hey!" the little man called out. "I'm a little man, not a bird. Don't you see? Don't you need a wish?" He cocked his head and shifted the great worm slung over his shoulder. "I guess not, huh? Oh well, my mistake." And he flew away with his worm.

Dan and Diana were getting set to go out to the garden just a bit later, when Diana thought about the robin again and she said, "You know, there was something strange about that bird. I've never seen a robin carry a worm over his shoulder like that before."

"Oh?" said Dan, looking down his hoe handle. "I hardly noticed."

Diana looked at him. "I just barely noticed," she said.

"In fact," said Dan, putting the hoe on his shoulder, "I didn't notice at all."

"Well, then," said Diana, "neither did I."

And out they went to hoe the garden together.

THE LOST
KINGDOM
OF
KARNICA

This was rejected twenty-four times. I thought it was a good story, nonetheless, but didn't know where else to send it. One friend thought it was about linguistics, another that it was about dark Freudian recesses, another that it was about ecology. The last notion seemed to have some market value, so I sent it to Sierra Club and they published it as their first children's book. It probably came from reading too much Kafka.

ALL THINGS were not especially fine or wonderful in the Kingdom of Karnica before the stone was found, but the land was rich and yielding, and there was work and food for the people and a pleasant life for most. The king had never had the temptation to do anything really evil or the opportunity to do anything fatally foolish. And of course he had a wise man to give him good advice. But life got worse, and quickly, after the stone was found.

The story of how the stone was found was told many hundreds of times in those last days, and the manner of it was this: Farmer Erd was digging a well, a very deep well because of his ordinary bad luck, when he struck into the stone with his pick. He tried for half a day to dig around it, but with no luck, for the stone was enormous. Then he went home to sleep on the problem.

The next day he got neighbor Grum to come help him. They took torches and tools to the bottom of the well. Farmer Erd had the idea that they could split the stone with a chisel and take it out in pieces. Grum held the chisel and Erd hit it with a sledgehammer. "Whank! Whank! Whank!"

"Don't hit my muckle-muckle hand!" Grum cussed.

"I wouldn't hit your muckle-muckle hand," Erd said.

"Whank! Whank! Whank!"

A few chips jumped up from the stone, but it wouldn't split. Erd wiped his brow. "What kind of muckle-muckle stone *is* that?" he said.

"I'll be muckle-muckle if I know," said Grum.

"Let's give it a look," said Erd, taking up his flask of water. He poured some water on the stone and rubbed at it with his shirttail. Soon they could see in the fluttering torchlight that they were kneeling on a smooth red stone. Rainbows of light shone from it and washed like surf across the surface and settled back in golden-red pools of internal fire. It was obvious even to Erd and Grum that this was a precious stone, and it was bigger than a horse.

The men gasped and breathed out in awe and reverence, "Muckle-*muckle!*"

Erd and Grum then took an oath and swore on their mothers' graves to keep this find a secret, and they chipped off from the stone what they figured would be about a thousand dollars worth of precious gemstones.

That evening Farmer Erd had a dinner and a party for every relative of his he could find, and there were fifty-three of them at dinner, and more showed up later. Neighbor Grum went to town and bought drinks several times in several public places, and both men paid their costs with the flickering red gems.

Everyone knew about the stone in the well by ten o'clock the next morning. And so did the King.

"I'll have a look at that," said the King. He was taken to the place upon his royal litter. He looked into the well, and his royal goldsmith and royal jeweler went down into the hole to make a close inspection. They came out of the hole with the report that the stone was precious and of the highest quality. The King told Erd and Grum that some King's men would assist in digging up the stone. He was lifted up in his litter, and he called out as the royal party left the place, "Dig it up! Jump to it!" And they jumped to it and began to dig up the stone right away.

The King's men worked all through the day while the news of the stone traveled around the kingdom. By dusk a thousand people had gathered to watch the working men who climbed in and out of the hole carrying dirt and water and tools. Washers and polishers were sent into the hole to make it shine like a jewel as it was being dug clear of the earth. The hole grew larger and a mound of dirt surrounded it. But the workers could not come to the edge of the stone, and at the end of the day the hole was forty feet across. Erd and Grum strutted about, telling their story and giving instructions that no one paid any attention to.

The King ordered on a night shift. That night he stood at a palace window and looked out across the darkened fair fields of Karnica to the mellow glow of torches where the stone lay. "Rich," he muttered, "rich!" A minister at his elbow leaned forward and said in his ear, "Indeed, Sire. We shall be the richest kingdom in the world . . . or elsewhere."

All night the King's men worked, and the next morning the day shift came on. By midday the hole was so large that the King ordered all those who had come to watch to go to their homes and return with picks, shovels and wheelbarrows, and they also went into the hole to work. The King himself moved to the site to give his personal attention to the labor. A banquet table was set up, and the King nibbled on grapes and dainties while attendants flocked about for his comfort's sake. They could hear him mutter under the linen napkin he dabbed to his mouth, "Rich, rich!" Several times the King was lifted in his chair and the banquet table was moved back to make room for the widening hole. The workers worked all that day and all that night.

On the third day of digging, Farmer Erd's barn and house and fences were torn down as the hole reached out like a whirlpool. And then neighbor Grum's farm was taken under, and then others. A circular hill of earth and debris grew up all about the hole, and there was no end yet to the great red stone.

The wise man of the kingdom had not been idle all this while. He had been thinking, and wondering, and he had been studying his books. For long hours he had stood on the edge of the hole and gazed into the depths of the stone, which seemed to him to burn with a living and moving fire. His thoughts went deep into this mystery, and at length he reached a conclusion.

Touching a knee before the King, and touching a hand to his breast, he said, "The stone is the heart of the kingdom."

The King paused between grapes, glanced at his minister, who smiled, and then the King said to the wise man, "Don't make me laugh."

In another day the royal treasury was half used up from hiring workers from neighboring kingdoms. The hole was now as big as sixty farms and four hundred fields, but there was no sign that the workers were coming to the edge of the stone. On the next day the royal treasury was completely used up, and the royal palace was torn down to make room for the hole. The people of the kingdom and the workers lived in tents around the edge of the hole, and torches and campfires blazed at night around the great circle like the rim of a volcano. Inside the royal tent the King could be heard muttering, "Rich, rich!"

The wise man, sitting in his tent with a few books and a candle, sent word to the King asking permission to see him again. He was received in the King's tent. The minister was rolling up a map, and looked at the wise man sidelong and suspiciously.

The wise man dropped to a knee before the King. "The stone is the heart of the kingdom," he said. "And if we remove it, the kingdom will die."

The minister grunted, and the King said, "That's just a lot of muckle-muckle. Go away."

That was exactly the wise man's intention. He went about that night to several encampments, and in the glowing blood-red light reflected from the stone he spoke his wisdom that it should be passed about as a warning to all. For his trouble, he received only scoffing and sarcasm. On the following day the wise man bundled his few belongings together and walked to the ocean shore. There he found a man with a boat who promised to keep his books dry, and they sailed to another land.

Lakes were emptied, forests were cut down and rivers were turned to spill over the stone and wash it. Many more workers were hired, and great machines were invented that could dig faster than men, and everything was paid for with pieces of the stone. The hooves of horses were tied about with layers of soft leather, and messengers galloped across the gleaming surface of the stone carrying instructions and messages. At night, the thudding rhythm of the horses galloping across the stone sounded like a heartbeat to those who lay quietly on the earth and who listened.

The dirt piled up all around the edge of the stone like a range of hills, and then the day came when the workers had reached the borders of the neighboring kingdoms, and yet the stone was solid in the earth. All the tents of the workers were crowded onto the ocean shore of the Kingdom of Karnica. The King could not dig into the other kingdom's lands, and besides, part of the stone would belong to them if he did so. He studied the situation carefully, and then gave his orders. "Yank it out! Yank the muckle-muckle thing out!"

But it is much easier to decide to yank a stone out of the ground than it is to yank it out. Because all the land of the kingdom was dug up, the workers would have to pull at the stone from the shore of the ocean, and from boats and ships out in the sea. Therefore, many hundreds of boats and ships were bought and built to do the work, and many fishermen and sailors and crabbers were hired to man the flotilla. More engineers were hired, and great winches were constructed on the beach to haul at the stone.

The plan was this: Long ropes were attached to the boats and ships, and to the winches on the shore, and then fastened to the stone in many inventive ways. It was hoped that all the hundreds of boats and ships and winches would lift the great red stone out of the earth on the outgoing tide and wind.

When the sun was on the horizon, the wind and tide swept out with a mighty lust, and the great red stone lifted from the earth and rolled over everyone on the beach and disappeared into the deeps, taking with it to the bottom of the ocean every boat and ship. The waters of the ocean crashed into the empty hole and caused a storm which lasted for six days.

Then it was quiet and still. And there now ebbs a dark sea where the heart of the Kingdom of Karnica was torn from the breast of the earth.

That is the end of the story. The place is gone, and the people are gone. We shall not hear of them again. Surely it is a muckle-muckle shame, but it is the muckle-muckle truth.

OLIVER HYDE'S DISHCLOTH CONCERT

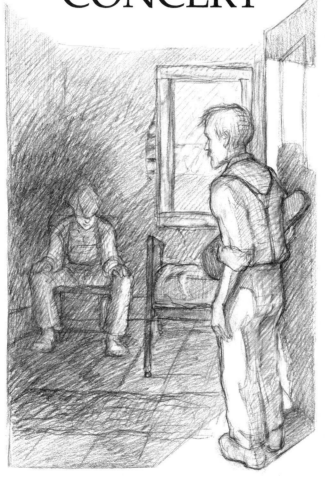

NOW maybe it's sad and maybe it's spooky, but there was a man who lived just out of town on a scrubby farm and no one had seen his face for years. If he was outside working, he kept his hat pulled down and his collar turned up, and if anyone approached him he ran up the hill to his house and shut himself inside. He left notes pinned to his door for a brave errand boy who brought him supplies from town. The people asked the boy what he heard up there in that tomblike house when he collected the notes and delivered the supplies. "Darkness and quietness," said the boy. "I hear darkness and quietness." The people nodded and looked at the boy. "Aren't you afraid?" The boy bit his lip. "A fellow has to make a living," he said.

Sometimes the children would come out of town and sing a little song up at the house and then run away. They sang:

> "The beautiful bride of Oliver Hyde,
> Fell down dead on the mountainside."

Yes, it was true. The man was full of grief and bitterness. He was Oliver Hyde, and his young bride's wagon had been washed into a canyon by a mudslide and it killed her, horse and all. But that was years ago. The children sang some more:

> *"Oliver Hyde is a strange old man,*
> *He sticks his head in a coffee can,*
> *And hides his face when there's folks about,*
> *He's outside in, and he's inside out."*

It was too bad. Oliver used to have many friends, and he played the fastest and sweetest fiddle in the county. And for the few short weeks he was married his playing was sweeter than ever. But on the day his wife was buried he busted his fiddle across a porch post, and now he sat cold, dark, and quiet on his little hill. No one had visited him for years. There was a reason. You shall see.

One day a man came from the town and walked up the hill toward Oliver's house. He was carrying a fiddle case. Two or three times he stopped and looked up at the house and shook his head, as if trying to free himself from a ghost, and continued on. He arrived at the porch steps. All the window shades were pulled down and it was dead quiet inside. The three porch steps creaked like cats moaning in their dreams, and the man knocked on the door. For a little bit it was quiet, then there was the sound of a chair being scooted across the floor. A voice said, "Come in."

The man opened the door a crack and peeked inside.

"Oliver?" he said. "It's me, Jim." No answer. Jim opened

the door farther and put a foot inside. It was dark, and smelled stale. Jim opened the door all the way.

Off in a corner where the light didn't touch sat a figure in a chair, perfectly upright, with his hands on his knees like a stone god, as still and silent as a thousand years ago. The head was draped completely with a dishcloth. Not a breath ruffled the ghost head.

Jim swallowed and spoke. "Haven't seen you around lately, Oliver." No answer.

People used to visit Oliver for a while after his beautiful bride fell down dead on the mountainside, but this is how it was—Oliver sitting in the dark with a dishcloth over his head, and he never spoke to them. It was too strange. His friends stopped visiting.

All Jim wanted was a single word from Oliver—yes or no. He had a favor to ask. He was Oliver's oldest friend. He moved inside.

"Sue's getting married, Oliver," he said. No answer. "You remember my little girl, Sue? She's all growed up now, Oliver, and mighty pretty, too." For all the notice he got, Jim might just as well have been talking to a stove. He cleared his voice and went on. "The reason I came, Oliver, was to ask you to come and play the fiddle for us at the dance. We was the best friends, and I don't see how I can marry off Sue without you being there to fiddle for us. You can just say yes or no, Oliver."

Now Oliver wasn't dead himself yet, so he still had feelings, and Jim had been his best friend. They had played and fought together, fished and hunted, and grown up together. So Oliver hated to say "No" just flat out like that, so he said instead, "No fiddle." Jim was prepared for that, and he laid the fiddle case down on the floor and flipped it open.

"Here, I brought a fiddle, Oliver. Porky Fellows was happy to make a lend of it."

Oliver felt trapped now. He was silent for a long time, then finally he said, "Tell you what. I can't wear this dish-cloth on my head and fiddle, but if everyone else wears a dishcloth I'll come."

Jim was quiet for a long time, but at last he said, "All right, Oliver, I'll ask if they'll do it. The dance is tomorrow night at Edward's barn. I'll leave the fiddle here, and if I don't come back to pick it up, then you got to come to the dance and fiddle for us. I got your promise."

Oliver smiled under his dishcloth. They'd be fools to agree to that. You can't have any fun with a dishcloth over your head.

"So long, Oliver," Jim said. Oliver didn't answer. Jim went back on down the hill.

Oliver took the dishcloth off. The fiddle was laying in the light of the open door. He sucked a whisker and looked at it. Oliver knew the fiddle, and it was a good fiddle. He wondered if it was in tune and wanted to pick it up, but he let it lay there. His foot was tapping, and he slapped his knee to make it stop. He laughed to himself and mut-tered, "Them donkeys—what do they know?" Then he got up and moved around the little house on his dreary business.

The sun went down and the shadow of the fiddle case stretched across the floor. Oliver's eyes kept landing on the fiddle, and he stepped over the shadow when he crossed that way. It looked to him like the bow had new horsehair on it. But it didn't make any difference to him. He figured he'd never be playing on that fiddle, and he never touched it.

Next morning Oliver watched down the hill for Jim to come and tell him the deal was off and to get the fiddle. Noon came. Oliver ate some beans. Afternoon came on. Jim didn't show. Oliver began to get mad. He was mad that he had ever made the promise. It started to get dark. "Those cluckheads!" Oliver said, pulling the window shut. "They can't dance with dishcloths on their heads, or drink punch, either. They'll have a rotten time."

But a promise is a promise.

Finally he decided it was time to put his hat and coat on. "They tricked me," Oliver grumbled, "but I got a trick for them, too. They'll be sorry I came to their party." It wasn't a great trick Oliver had in mind, but just a miserable little one to make sure nobody could have any fun while he was there. He figured they'd ask him to leave shortly. He wouldn't even bother to take off his hat and coat.

He headed down the hill with the fiddle and into the little town. He entered Edward's barn with his hat pulled down and his collar turned up. It was dark except for two bare, hanging light bulbs, one over the center of the barn and one at the end where a sort of stage was built up. Oliver had played at shindigs there many times. He kept his head down, and only from the corners of his eyes could he see all the people sitting around the walls. "Lord, it's awfully dark," Oliver thought to himself, "and quiet. I figure they know that's the way I like it." He got under the light bulb that hung over the stage and took out the fiddle.

He tuned down to a fretful and lonesome sound, and then he played.

Of course he knew they were all looking for happy dancing tunes, so first off he played a slow and sad tune about a man who was walking down a long road that had no ending and was gray all about, and the man was looking forward to being dead because it might be more cheerful. Nobody danced, naturally, and didn't clap either when Oliver finished it. "That's just right," Oliver thought. "I'll give them a wretched time." And he started on another.

The second tune he played was even slower and sadder, about a man who thought his heart was a pincushion and it seemed to him that everyone was sticking pins and needles into it, and it was hurtful even to listen to it. Nobody danced, and nobody even moved to the punch bowl to get their spirits up. "Now they're sorry I came," Oliver thought. Still, he had played that last tune especially sweet, and he expected someone might have clapped a little just for that, even if it was sad.

Oliver looked out a little under his hat as he retuned a bit. He tried to see Jim. He ought to come up and say hello at least, not just let him stand there completely alone. And he wondered where the other musicians were. Four people were sitting down off to the right of the stage. That would be them. Oliver considered it would be nice to have a little slide guitar on these slow ones, sort of mournful played, and a mouth harp and mandolin would fit in nice. "Naw! This is just the way I want it. One more gloomy song and they'll ask me to leave."

So then he played another, this one about a man who had a wife that just recently moved to heaven, and how roses grew all over her tombstone even in the winter. Oliver was halfway through that before he remembered that he'd played that tune at his own wedding party. He pulled up short a bit then, but kept on playing it out, and a tear rolled down his cheek. Well, nobody could see. He wiped his eyes when he was finished.

Nobody clapped and nobody moved, just sat against the dark walls perfectly still. Among the dark figures was a lighter shape. Probably the bride in her white gown. Oliver remembered how lovely and happy his bride had been, and he felt a little mean when he thought about that, giving out such sad tunes.

He spoke out loud, the first words that were spoken since he came in. "Well, I guess you're all ready for me to leave now, and I will. But first I want to play just one happy tune for the bride, and so you can dance, and then I'll go." Then he did play a happy one, a fast one, carrying on with fiddling lively enough to scramble eggs. But nobody got up to dance, and when he was finished nobody moved or made a sound.

"Look here," Oliver said. "I reckon you can't dance with those dishcloths over your heads, I forgot about that. So take 'em off. I'll give you another dancing tune, then I'll go." And then he went into another, as sweet and light and fast as anyone ever could, something to get even a rock up and dancing, but nobody moved. And when he was finished they all sat silent with the dishcloths still on their heads.

"Come on," Oliver said. "Take those things off your

heads. You other fellows get up here with your music and help me out. Let's have some dancing, drink some punch, let's get alive now." He stomped his foot three times and threw into a tune that would churn butter all by itself. But the other four musicians sat perfectly still, and so did everybody else, and Oliver was standing there under the light bulb in silence when he finished the tune.

He stood there with his head down, understanding things, and how it felt to be on the other side of the darkness and silence when all you wanted was some sign of life to help out. Then he leaned over and put the fiddle in the case and closed it. He said one last thing, then walked out from under the light toward the door. "Okay," he said. "That's a hard lesson, but I got it."

When he opened the door he bumped into someone sitting next to it against the wall, and the fellow fell off his chair. Oliver put a hand down to help him up. But the fellow just lay there. Oliver touched him. "What's this?" He felt around, then shoved back his hat for a look. It was a sack of grain he'd knocked over. And the next person sitting there was a sack of grain, too. And the next was a bale of hay.

Oliver walked completely around the barn. All the people were sacks of grain and bales of hay sitting against the dark walls, and the bride was a white sack of flour. The four musicians sitting off to the right of the stage were four old saddles setting on a rail.

When Oliver came around to the door again he heard music. He stepped outside and looked down the street. A barn down near the end was all lit up, and lots of people were moving about. He went back up on the stage, got the fiddle, and headed down the street.

Jim was standing by the door. "Waiting for you, Oliver," he said. "We're just getting under way—come on in." When he led Oliver inside everyone became quiet, first one little group of people then another, until at last everyone was silent and looking at Oliver. The bride and groom were holding hands. Jim made a motion and everyone headed for a chair against the walls. They all took out dishcloths to put over their heads.

"Edward's got himself a new barn, huh?" Oliver said.

"Yeah," said Jim. "I guess you didn't know that. Uses the old one to store stuff. I shoulda told you."

"It's all right," Oliver said. He looked up on the stage. Four musicians were sitting there with dishcloths over their heads. Then Jim took out a large dishcloth. Oliver touched him on the arm.

"Never mind that. And everyone else, too. Just be regular and dance. I'll fiddle for you."

Jim slapped him on the back and shouted out the good news. Oliver went up on the stage. Someone got him a mug of punch. The musicians tuned up. Oliver took off his hat and dropped it, and tossed his coat on a chair. They lit into a fast, happy tune. They danced and played and sang half the night.

Ah, they had a wonderful time. Oliver included.

THE
MOUSE GOD

I picked up a hitchhiker who was dressed in trousers, shirt, and jacket all made up of scraps of leather sewn tightly together. His subject was Almighty God, and we took a long, fair ride up the Yaquina Bay road to the Pacific. Years later I discovered that since that time I had been collecting scraps of leather, and had a whole box full of them, for whatever use I haven't the slightest idea.

THERE WAS a large barnyard cat who was both vain and lazy, and he would have preferred of all things to lie upon a windowsill in the sun and love himself. But he had to earn his keep, so each day he attended to chasing mice and sent a good number of them off to eternity. The constant hunting was a terror to the mice, but also a grief to the cat, for he mussed and dirtied his fine coat as he chased his quarry under the floorboards, across the roof beams, and through all manner of grimy and dusty places. He had a small mirror to look into, and it distressed him awfully to come back to the shed he lived in and find his fur so tangled and dirty. It sometimes took him half a day after a chase to put his fur in order again, and he would sit on his windowsill licking at himself and hating the mice, for he blamed them that he did not have enough leisure time to himself.

And then one night he awoke in the middle of a dream. "Why, yes!" he said. He had the solution. "I will only need some coveralls such as the farmer wears, and that way I shall remain practically clean no matter where I must chase the mice." He went to sleep again, and in the morning over his bowl of milk he concluded his plans. He would begin saving mouse skins to make himself a sleek coat that he could move about in as quickly and smoothly as in his own coat of fur. This way he would keep his own fur clean. Once a week he could wash out the mouse coat in the creek and save several hours of his own time each day. He could spend this time napping and admiring himself in his mirror.

And so it was that the cat began catching the mice by their heads so as to save their skins in one piece, and he got salt and alum to cure the tiny pelts, and he pinned them to the wall of the shed to dry. In a month's time he had enough pelts to make himself a coat. He took needle and thread then, and sitting cross-legged in the corner of the shed, he began working on the garment.

"Pockets inside or out?" he wondered as he worked and planned on the coat. "Inside, to be sure, so they won't snag on anything in the chase." He worked on, sewing the pelts together. "Shall it have a belt?" He thought on this for a while. "Yes, a belt to tighten the coat when I scramble through small places, that is a good idea." He sewed on. "A collar? Yes, a collar of course, to snug up close around my ears in cold weather. And shall I make it with a zipper down the front, or with buttons? Hmmmmmmm. Buttons will do." And he continued sewing on his mouse-skin coat, and presently had it all finished.

He put it on and stood in front of his mirror. It fit beautifully. "Stylish," said the cat, turning this way and that. He found that he had enough mouse skins left over for a pair of boots, so he finished those and looked at himself again. "Dainty," he said, pointing his toes. Still there was more fur left, so he made himself a hat. He made it with a brim, and also earflaps. "It will keep the cobwebs out of my ears," said the cat, and he looked at himself again. "Smart!" he said, and he picked up a sparrow feather and stuck it in the hat. He looked again, and winked at himself. "Why, the hat should set a fashion all by itself," he said. Then he went out on the hunt.

The coat and boots and hat hardly hindered him at all, and he came upon a mouse around a corner of the barn and set himself to spring at the creature as soon as it should recover from its fright. But the mouse only lay there on the ground, staring with its little eyes wide open. The cat was quite a sight. He stood perfectly still also, for those are the rules of a cat-and-mouse chase. The mouse must run first. But the mouse did not run. When it had quite gotten over its awe, it called out, "Friends, cousins, brothers, sisters! Come out, come out! The Mouse God has come to visit us!"

Well! And yet you know, it might be imagined—a large cat covered all over with mouse skins just might be mistaken for a Mouse God. The cat understood this at once, and waited perfectly still to see what else should come of the matter. Then other mice appeared, and in great wonder at the sight of the cat in his mouse coat, they lay down all around him in reverence until at last the cat was surrounded by dozens of mice, all of them waiting for the Great Mouse God to break his silence.

Now, the cat saw that he had come upon a wonderful

opportunity if only he could use it right. It would not do to run among the mice. He might catch a half-dozen of them, but if he played his role of the Mouse God cleverly, he might get them all at a single catch. Therefore, he thought carefully and came up with his plan. He addressed the mice thus:

"Children, I have been watching you from heaven, and although you are good mice, you could be better. And so I have come to set you on the path that will surely lead you to heaven. Do you wish to go to heaven?"

"Oh, yes," cried the mice, "we all wish to go to heaven."

"Good," said the cat. "Then you must go to church, and you must praise me and sing hymns."

"But we have no church," the mice said.

"Then you must build one," said the cat. "Over there is a large crate. That will do quite nicely. Clean it out, make a wide door, put benches in it, and paint it white. And when I come around on next Sunday morning, I expect to find all of you inside singing hymns."

"Shall we make a steeple for it?"

"Naturally," said the cat.

"And colored glass for the windows?"

"Exactly," said the cat. "And you shall all be well on your way to heaven by next Sunday. Now go home and meditate on the job before you, and I will go back to heaven."

The mice ran off, and the cat crept back to his shed. Later in the day the mice got busy making the old crate into a church, and the cat watched out of his window.

The mice worked that day and all the next, which was

Saturday, and the cat lay lazily on his sill and watched them. The church was coming along nicely. Near the end of the day the mice moved the benches in, and then they painted the crate white. The cat went to his supply chest and got out a length of rope and tested its strength by tugging at a doorknob. "This should do," he said.

The next morning it was Sunday, and the cat watched while all the mice filed solemnly into their fine and bright new church. The steeple pointed to heaven and the colored windows sparkled in the sun. The cat put on his coat and boots and hat, and when he heard the mice singing hymns, he took his piece of rope and went out to the church. He listened for a while to the mice singing for their salvation, and he smiled. His plan was to throw the rope around the crate and drag it to the bridge over the river and dump it in, thus to be done with the mice forever. He knocked on the roof of the crate. "That's very nice singing, my children, and it makes me happy to know you are all in church."

"Is that you, God?" they cried.

"Oh, yes," said the cat, throwing the rope around the crate and tightening it over the doors. Then he took the rope over his shoulder and began dragging the crate toward the bridge.

"Where are you taking us, God?" the mice cried out.

"To heaven, my children, straight to heaven. Sing bravely, now."

And the mice continued to sing as the cat lurched forward on his rope and dragged the crate up the road toward the bridge. At last he had the crate on the bridge. He looped the rope twice more around the crate and knotted it over the doors. Then he prepared to lift it over the rail and dump it in the river. The mice sang:

"We all love you, if you please;
give to us our daily cheese."

The cat struggled with the crate but could not find a good grip on it. Besides that, it was too heavy for him to lift. He set the corner down and wondered what to do. The mice sang:

"We all sing and praise you that
you will save us from the cat."

Along came a closed wagon, and it rumbled up onto the bridge. On the side of the wagon were written in colorful paints such things as these:

ISAIAH 12:5
LUKE 12:32
MATTHEW 19:14
LUKE 17:21
23RD PSALM

For these are references to the Bible, and this was the wagon of an old traveling preacher. When the wagon was opposite the crate and the cat, the old man pulled up his horse and listened to the mice singing hymns in their pretty soprano voices.

"Young man," said the preacher to the cat (he did not see too well), "that is the most astounding music box I have ever heard. And how clever, to have it made to look just like a small church. I would give a good amount to have such a thing for myself, for I am not able to offer the faithful any music of my own."

The mice began another hymn.

The cat considered. "Do you travel far?" he asked the preacher.

"Clear across the country," said the old man. "From one end of the land to the other, spreading the good word and teaching righteousness."

The cat thought on this. If he gave the crate to the old preacher, the mice would be gone forever. That would be as good as drowning them.

"The box is yours," said the cat. "Remember me in your prayers."

The preacher loaded the crate into the back of his wagon and started on his way again. He waved to the cat, and called out, "Thanks be to God."

"You're welcome," said the cat.

And that is the end of the story for the cat. He went back to his shed and lay down on the windowsill in the sun.

As for the mice, they stopped singing after a while and cried out, "Are we in heaven yet?" The preacher went around to the back of his wagon and threw off the rope from the crate and opened the doors. He was quite surprised that it was not a music box, but a box filled with singing mice, yet he was not at all disappointed. He took care not to frighten the small creatures, and fed them some cheese. In the next few days he built them little tables and chairs and beds, and gave them a whole half of his wagon to live in. He let them run in the fields and kept them safe and set out as good meals for them as he did for himself, and they lived happily together.

When the people gathered around the wagon to hear the old man preach, the mice went into the crate and sang hymns, so many people were fortunate to hear their sweet voices. Now and then they would ask the old preacher if they were in heaven yet.

"Are you not happy?" asked the old man.

"Very happy," said the mice.

"Then you are in heaven," said the preacher. "Sing 'amen,' children."

"*Aaaaaaa . . . men,*" sang the mice.

Amen.

INSIDE MY FEET
The Story of a Giant

Two A.M. I am alone in a large aquarium doing my job as a janitor. The fish, silent and ponderous, watch me from behind thick glass. And there in the middle of the spacious, clear floor is a very large pair of black dress shoes. I take them to the office. Lost and found. No one ever claimed them. Out there in the world, somewhere, there is a very big man walking about barefoot, trying to remember where he left his shoes. Lucky if you don't meet him.

WHEN I was a child we lived on a lonely road near the edge of a forest where the darkness went in forever like a bottomless lake. Our nearest neighbor was out of sight and sound, and I remember always one night when both my father and mother were carried off down that road into that deep forest. Then I was left alone in the house waiting to be carried off myself. This is the story of that night, which was a bad night, and of the next night, which was worse.

I awoke at midnight as if someone had called my name, but the room was empty and I had not even the vanishing tail of a dream to remind me why I had come awake. I listened deeply. The house and all about was quiet. The steady silence of the moonlight fell on my bed and cast the outline of my window across the floor. Something was strange, but I couldn't sense what it was. Something was wrong, and something was waiting. The seconds counted slowly by like notes in a funeral dirge. I listened and watched the dark corners of my room. Underneath my bed was a large and cold hand that also watched, and waited for me to dangle a naked arm or leg over the side so it could drag me screaming into that dark pit where it would rip and smother me until I was dead, and torment me afterward. But there was nothing unusual in that. It had been waiting since I was five. Something else was waiting . . . some terror unknown to me.

When I was younger I would have got out of bed (careful to avoid the hand) and gone right to my folks' room across the hall, there to climb in bed and lie between the warm mountains of my mother and father, safe in the shadow and small valley of myself. But now I was older, and those easy nights were gone. I must listen and watch alone when the darkness called my name. I could hear my father snoring softly. My mother made a gentle moan.

Leaning forward in my bed, I looked out my upstairs window into the sky, and saw the giant. It was not a real giant, but a giant made up of stars. He stalks across the night sky with bears and dragons and dogs, with gods and goddesses, snakes and goats, and other things that live in the sky. When he was alive he was a great hunter, but now his spirit lives in the heavens. Orion is his name. I knew him best by the belt he wears, clearly made up of three bright stars, the names of which are so ancient that scarcely anyone can pronounce them anymore. This mighty hunter Orion carries a club and a sword and eternally hunts the Milky Way, sinking feet first into the western horizon in the early morning. I marked his place in the sky, and so I knew the time. "Just about midnight," I whispered to myself. I settled back into bed, sorry that I had asked. It might have been a better time. Then came the knock from downstairs at our front door.

It was not the clear and candid knock of a visiting neighbor or friend, nor yet the deliberate thumping of a stranger seeking help or direction. Rather, it was a shuffling and uncertain call, as if from a creature who was wounded, or deeply ashamed, a curious sliding and falling away ghost of a knock. But something more was curious as well. Our dog, Harley, had not barked. That was certainly strange. I heard my father get out of bed. I was at my bedroom door across from my folks' room when he came out. He was barefooted, wearing his nightshirt, with a shotgun in his hand. The shotgun was a side-by-side double-barrel 8-gauge with twin triggers. It was our bird gun, but up close it would do for an elephant. It was also used to investigate the rare midnight visitors who came down our road, far past the last humming electric wire. Father carried a lantern in the other hand. He motioned with his head for me to stay where I was. Three steps took him to the head of the stairs. He hesitated, and stepped down. Mother came to the door, pulling on her robe.

Very softly, I said, "Harley didn't bark." She looked at me and nodded, a deep nod descending into old memories and eerie stories I had sometimes heard. Mother had a feeling for these things that father lacked. Father would have said of Harley, "Probably sick." Mother would be more inclined to suggest that he had been changed into a wheelbarrow or something. For father, the world was a straightforward and everyday business until it was proved to be strange or mysterious. As for mother, the world was strange and mysterious until it was proved to be straightforward and everyday business. But more of this later.

A stair creaked and we heard nothing else till the sound of father sliding the bolt on the front door and lifting the latch. For a few moments it was silent. A breath died slowly in my lungs. Then father called up to us.

"Come take a look at this!"

Mother went down first, and I followed in the billow of her robe. Father had moved around a bit and bolted the door by the time we got there. No one else was in the room, and nothing was out of order that we could see. Mother said, "What was it, dear?" Father lifted the lantern slightly, looking past us toward the floor. "They were outside," he said.

I turned and looked. There on the floor was a pair of boots, common in all ways as any honest countryman's boots, except that they were as long as one of my arms, deep enough to hide a bread box in, past all size numbers, boots with leather enough in them to cover a small chair—the boots of a giant! My father rubbed his chin. As I have said, he took strict care of his imagination. He might admit that the weather was strange, but little else. He was a plain man, and reduced the world to the most simple and practical explanations available. Sometimes there is comfort in that, but it seemed to me completely out of place that he should now say, "Looks like somebody left their boots. Big fellow. I suppose he'll be back for them later." I was relieved, though, that he checked all the window latches before we started back upstairs, and left the room lighted by the lantern he had brought down.

"Harley didn't bark," I said to him. Father stopped with a foot on a step and considered this for a moment.

"Must be sick," he said.

"Or maybe a butter churn," mother muttered. Father raised an eyebrow at her. We went upstairs and got into our beds.

I could hear mother talking to father in the other room. Her remarks—about the boots no doubt, and possibly butter churns—were punctuated by father's agnostic grunts. I bundled a blanket about myself and sat cross-legged on the bed, looking out the window. I couldn't see the front path from that side of the house. I studied the shadow at the east side of the barn. It was a shadow large enough to hide a giant. But nothing moved or glinted there. The star giant Orion walked quietly over my head. My folks stopped talking, yet I knew that my mother was awake and watching and wondering like myself. I could feel it. And then there came the sound downstairs of someone walking about in boots.

Both mother and father were at their door as quickly as I was at mine. The walking about had been no more than three or four steps, and now had stopped. Father held the shotgun in both hands now, not with a loose strolling bird-hunting grip, but with a hold and touch meant for bear. Whoever it was downstairs, if he wished to remain warm-blooded, would be wise to stand perfectly still for a while longer. Father gave me a stern look and started downstairs. Mother and I waited, and listened.

The next thing we heard was the sound of walking about again. It was not father, but again somebody in boots. And it was not a casual walking about, but a sort of dancing step we heard. This stopped after a few steps and we heard a voice. A flat and weathered voice, not father's voice, a sort of slapping sound that loose bootlaces might make, with a lilting quality about it, almost like singing. But it said little, and as abruptly as it stopped father gave a whoop, and we heard a clatter of something heavy dropped on the floor. Immediately then the boots began stomping and the voice spoke again. The next moment the front door was flung open and banged on its hinges, and at last Harley began yelping as somebody ran down the front path. Mother and I stumbled down the stairs.

When we ran through the front room we noticed only that father was not there. The door was wide open and Harley was down by the fence barking. We ran down there without even a stick for a weapon, hopping in our bare feet when we stepped on sharp stones. The dog would not go past the fence; a piece of nightshirt was caught on a rail splinter where father had crossed over. We could hear boots running up the roadway, then the crashing of brush, and then it was quiet and cold and we were alone. I looked at mother. Her eyes were intent on the dark road, and the moon lit lines and muscles in her face that I had never noticed before. Harley was whining and looking for solace between our legs. After a minute, mother made a decision. "Back to the house," she said, and we ran back.

On the floor was the shotgun where father had dropped it, or where it had been torn from his hands. Mother bolted the front door and took up the gun. She checked both chambers to make certain it was loaded, then walked around thumping her fist to each window latch to make certain it was closed tight.

"What was it?" I asked. "What happened?"

Mother only shook her head and said, "Upstairs—in my room." I climbed into my folks' bed, on her side, and she sat up in my father's place and leaned the shotgun against the side table. She lit a lamp and sat upright with her arms folded, looking at the door. I lay in the warm and strange smells of the bed and watched her face.

Father could tell stories about winters when it snowed up past the windows, and of a yard-long fish he had caught, and how his grandfather had been chased by Indians, and about the time he fell twenty feet out of a tree and wasn't even hurt, and of the birth of twin calves, and that was all exciting, of course. My mother's side of the family was different. Mother knew other kinds of stories. Mother told about a time it snowed *red* snow, and of a fish *her* father caught with a gold watch in it, still ticking, and how her grandfather had returned from woodcutting in the forest with a wound, a deep scar across his forehead, and how ever after he could say only one single word, and only that one word, until the day he died. Unfortunately, mother could not remember what the word was. And she told about the time Cousin Floyd fell out of a tree with a yell, and when those nearby went to help him he was gone and never heard from again, and about the birth of a calf with two heads.

And as mother was full of mystery and dark things, so

also was she strangely innocent of the effect of these stories on me. One evening she told me about a dead man who had been found in their root cellar when she was a little girl. He was sitting upright with a half-eaten jar of cherries in his lap. No one knew who he was, or how he had come to be there, or how he had died. "He was as cold as this stone," mother whispered, touching a stone on the fireplace. I wouldn't go to bed that night, and I cried. Mother tried to comfort me. "Just don't think about it, dear," she said. Just don't think about it, dear. . . . Ah, mother! For a long time afterward I kept an eye on that stone, and would not stand or sit within touching distance of it, and feared—as I would fear a dead man—to be in that room alone.

And so whatever this business of the boots was about, it seemed that mother might handle the situation better than father. It was her kind of story. But whatever mother knew, or was considering, she did not tell me. After a while I closed my eyes. Then I slept.

I was awake before the sound of a knock at our door had died in the corners. Mother slid from the bed and took up the lamp. Tucking the stock of the shotgun under her arm, she gave me a cautious look and went out the door. When she was gone into the darkness, I tiptoed to the door and watched the lamplight rolling on the walls as she went down the stairs. Again for a while it was quiet. The light that shone on the stairwell walls was steady now. Mother was at the front door.

"Who is it?" Mother called. "Who's there?" No answer. Mother slipped the bolt and opened the door. In a few seconds she raised her voice to me. "Come," she said. She was bolting the door when I got downstairs. We stood in the light of the lamp, and she pointed toward the floor with the shotgun. "They were on the doorstep," she said. There they were again, the same monstrous boots. Whoever could fit into them could rest his elbow on the eave of our porch. Mother held the shotgun on the boots and walked around them. I noticed she took care not to step on their shadows. Then she got the lamp and looked inside them, nodded, and hummed to herself. Finally she cradled the shotgun in her arm, and said to me, "Did I ever tell you about your Uncle Oscar and that hat he found?"

I shook my head.

"He found it alongside the road, a perfectly good hat, and he wore it for weeks before he just happened to turn out the hatband one day, and do you know what was inside that hatband?"

"No," I whispered.

Mother nodded wisely. "No one else knows, either, except for your Uncle Oscar. He took the hat and chopped it up into tiny pieces and buried it in the backyard."

I nodded, wide-eyed.

"But he went crazy anyway," said mother. "Come. Upstairs."

"But . . ." I said, hoping she would not leave this crazy mystery of my crazy Uncle Oscar disturbing every hat I should ever after see so that I should ever after be turning out hatbands before I dared to put a hat on my head.

"Never mind," mother said. "Don't think about it. Upstairs now." And we returned to bed.

Mother sat with the shotgun in her lap now, two pillows bunched up at her back, and I lay with my eyes wide open looking at her. Her eyes were set at some far distance, and her expression was grim. How strange, that I had lived with her all my life and I didn't know if she had ever killed anyone. It might be something a son would know about his mother. Perhaps this was not a good time to ask. Her face was as set and steady as an old photograph, and only the flickering light of the table lamp gave it any movement or life. I did not expect that she would make the same mistake as father, whatever that was. Her right thumb stroked the walnut stock of the shotgun, and she watched. We were expecting a visitor.

Twenty minutes passed. Then came a sound from below— the sound of somebody walking about in boots. Yet we had not heard a sound before that, either of the door being opened or of the windows being tried. Mother eased out of bed. She was frightened, but at her center she had the fortitude of a hitching post, and her whole courage was summoned up by the time she looked at me and with a shake of her head indicated that I should stay in the room. The walking about had stopped, and mother went out and around the corner. I listened the next few seconds in a silence that could have filled a dozen libraries. Mother had time to reach the bottom of the stairs. I tiptoed out to the hallway again. And then again there came the sound of the boots.

At the very first step I expected the blast of the double-barreled shotgun to announce that my mother had killed someone. But there was no blast, and the sound of the boots was not the apologetic and contrite step of someone caught on the other end of an 8-gauge shotgun. Again it was rather like a dancing step, an irregular hopping step with a sort of rhythm. And when the dancing stopped, there came the same voice as before, chanting or singing a sort of rhyme, though I could not make out the words. Then, "Crash!" I knew that mother had let go the shotgun, and she gave a yell the same as father, and as quick as that the boots began stomping toward the door. The strange voice spoke again, the door was thrown open, and everything went outside.

I ran downstairs. Harley was yelping at someone on the path. "Mother!" I cried. I got the shotgun from where mother had dropped it and hurried down the path. Harley was at the fence, barking up the roadway, but he would not follow. "Mother!" I yelled. I could not see the boots, but I heard them running, well up the roadway. Then they turned into the woods. I could hear the brush being crushed. Harley was moaning, eager to get back to the house. It was no good trying to get him to go with me up the roadway, and I would not go alone. I stood there for a while in the cold, biting my lip, wondering what to do. At last I fired off both barrels of the shotgun for lack of a better idea, and ran back to the house.

I brought Harley inside with me, since he had been of no use outdoors, and I latched and bolted the door. I took two cartridges from the box on the mantel and loaded the shotgun again. It was five hours or so till first light. Weird and uncanny long-dead ancestors from my mother's side of the family whispered in my ear, and I knew what I knew.

The boots were coming back for me. Somebody or something meant to carry us all off, and I was next. This was the way things were done. I had heard of such stories. One fine day a family is missed at the Saturday market. A couple of men ride out to see what ails them, and they find only an empty house, perhaps a pot of stew still brewing over the fire, no sign of violence or struggle and not a soul around, and the family is never seen nor heard of again. How long I had I didn't know, but I did not intend to go the same way as father and mother. Now came the practical and shrewd voices of the ancestors from my father's side of the family, and I began to make preparations.

First of all I got more light in the front room—three lamps in all—and I set them around to best light the dark corners. Keeping the shotgun near at hand always, I then got hammer and nails and nailed three large nails into the jamb of the front door and bent them over with the claw of the hammer. Then I got a ball of twine and, using the nails for eyes, looped three lengths of twine around them and attached the ends to the bolt, the door latch, and the handle. I took the loose ends back to the center of the room and moved a kitchen chair to that spot. Measuring the distance just so, I cut the twine, took the ends in hand, and sat down facing the door. I had built and designed rabbit snares, and this was no more difficult a problem. I tested my work. Pulling on the first length of twine, I slipped the bolt of the door. I pulled the next and the latch lifted. Taking up the shotgun into the crotch of my arm, I pulled the last length of twine and the door swung open. And I had a perfect, clear shot out the door, smack into somebody's oblivion. I rebolted the door and led my twine back to the chair. I was ready. I looked at the clock above the stove. It was nearly 2 A.M. I was wide awake. Harley was already sleeping by the fireplace, although the fire was out. I looked at the door and tried not to think of my mother's side of the family.

The way I had it figured was this: Whoever left the boots was quick to get away before he was caught. Perhaps then he hid around the side of the house, or maybe in the shadow of the barn. Since it took some time to come down from upstairs, it was safe for him to knock as he pleased and then hide. But I intended to catch him on the doorstep this time. At the first knock, before our visitor had a chance to step out of the boots or set them down, I would pull my twine and have the door open on him. And I, a safe distance away, was going to blow him to memories if he made a move to run off. If he wanted to live, he would stand, and he would take me to my mother and father. If I had to kill him, I would go into the forest in the morning alone and track the boots' path and rescue my folks.

An hour passed, but yet I stayed awake. I grew thirsty, but didn't want to leave the chair for a second. Harley grumbled in his sleep. I wondered if this thing wanted our dog, too. And why did it want us, after all? We were simple countryfolk. We had done no one any harm. Well, soon enough I might learn. My turn was coming.

I was just looking away from the clock when the first touch of a knock came at the door. Quickly then, one, two, three . . . the bolt slid, the latch lifted, the door opened, and I was ready. But there was no one there. Harley awoke and started to growl toward the door, but then he stopped and cringed back toward the fireplace. The boots were on the doorstep, sitting . . . waiting. Carefully, I moved to the door, shotgun ready, and looked outside. No one, and no sound at all. I grabbed the boot tops and hefted them inside. I bolted the door, set the boots a fair distance from the chair and studied the situation.

This was very puzzling. How had the visitor gotten away so quickly? The last knock had hardly sounded at the door when I yanked it open. How could he have gotten away so cleanly? Yet there was a greater puzzle to all this. That was, how was he going to get inside the house now? How had he got in the last two times, with the door bolted and the windows locked? I looked at the door and mused on this. Perhaps he had a magnet to move the bolt and latch of the door from the outside. Or perhaps a piece of wire was slipped inside to slide the bolt and 'lift the latch. Or . . . with an accomplice? Yes, an accomplice—a tiny one, who came down the chimney and opened the door for the giant! I jerked my head to the fireplace in a panic. Not much time had gone since I had let the boots in, and I quickly had a fire going in the fireplace. No one would enter that way. It was a comfort to Harley, but not to me. I reconsidered. If someone small had come down the chimney to let in this giant, then there would have been tracks of ashes and soot on the floor. And there were none. No. Whatever it was had to come in by the door.

I turned in my chair away from the boots and faced the door. My attention settled on the bolt. I cocked one hammer of the shotgun. If that bolt moved a hair, we were going to have need of a new door. At this distance the 8-gauge could make sawdust of an outhouse. The fire was welcome, like the touch of a friend at my side. Five minutes slowly passed. I watched that bolt so intently that I could have detected an earthquake in Argentina by its movement. But such a narrow focus of attention is surrounded all about with desolation and weariness, and my imagination drifted. I wondered about Uncle Oscar and the hat. It must have been a piece of paper in the hatband, to lie so flat. What did it say? Or maybe a picture? My eyes burned. I blinked, then closed them for just one moment to refresh them. Two moments passed. Ten passed. I popped my eyes open. I had nearly been asleep. I thumped my head and thrust my back into the chair.

The touch of the fire was now like a full arm thrown about me, and the length of my body was pressed with warmth and comfort. My head jerked back now and then from small ventures into sleep. The shotgun was too heavy to hold up, so I settled the butt of it on the chair between my legs and let the barrel lean on my shoulder, but kept my finger on the trigger. I nodded into sleep, each nod a little longer, each time coming back a little less near the surface of wakefulness, until finally my chin sank on my chest, and so I was asleep.

I slept like a log, but not the whole log. A twig of me was yet awake and taking notice of things. That twig was my finger on the trigger of the shotgun. When the first footstep came to the room I pulled the trigger and blew a hole in the roof large enough to let in the Last Judgment. And the explosion of it, being right below my nodding head, made me kick over backward in the chair and tumble half deafened and stunned onto the floor. Harley was letting out a terrible cry as I scrambled to a wall, shotgun still in hand, ears pounding, eyes blinking, throat full of smoke, expecting any second to be lifted off the ground by the giant and carried stomping out the front door. I rolled twice and turned, getting an elbow under myself, and aimed the gun to where the boots had last been. I had one shot left.

The first thing I could clearly see was Harley, who had now stopped barking and was staring in awe and horror at the boots. Then he retired under a table to let me carry out my argument with the boots on my own. They were dancing! No one was in them, and they were dancing! I kicked the chair aside to see them better, and glanced at the door. It was closed and bolted. The boots were all by themselves, dancing around in a circle. Well, then, the giant was invisible and could walk through walls. I aimed the shotgun above the boots to about where a giant's stomach would be.

"Stop!" I yelled.

The boots paid no heed to my command, and continued dancing in that circle. I sighted down the barrel of the shotgun. Whatever or whoever was in those boots had just half a second of existence left to them on my schedule, but then the boots, after having danced three times in a circle, *did* stop. I stood up and tried to make out whatever form was standing in them, but it was plain air to me. Then the tongues of the boots began clapping back and forth, and the boots *talked*! This is what they said:

"Inside my bones,
Inside my meat,
Inside my heart,
Inside my FEET!"

This little rhyme was so mixed up in its sound with mystery, and time, and memory, and sadness, that I stood listening almost in a trance. But the very last word, FEET, was pronounced with such power and willfulness, that *my* feet responded: *they jumped into the boots!* This was without my will—my feet jumped and took me with them. I had no desire to jump into those boots at all. It was as if a puppeteer's strings were tied to my knees. I could do nothing but obey those invisible sinews of another's will. And my feet jumped with such a force of obedience that I was flung out—back arched, arms thrown wide—and wrenched so suddenly and violently that the shotgun was thrown from my grip. I found myself planted solidly, captured securely in those giant boots. Then I began stomping toward the door!

I should say, rather, that I was *carried* stomping to the door, for I had no control at all in the matter. My knees lifted and my legs moved totally against my will. *This* was how my folks had been carried off, and now I was being carried off myself. In two moments we were at the door, and then I saw the mistake my mother and father had made. If I was to be carried away, the door would first have to be opened. They should never have opened the door, and I determined that rather than let the boots take me outside

I would let them bang and beat me against that bolted door until I fell down unconscious or dead. But when we got to the door, the boots stopped, and spoke another rhyme:

> *"Open wide and you will see*
> *What shall become of you and me.*
> OPEN WIDE!"

Now—again against my will—in full obedience to the command of the boots, my hands darted up and I threw the bolt and flung the door open. I could not have done otherwise. Then we ran out and down the pathway. Harley came barking after, of no use for anything *but* barking, and he wasn't sure he wanted to get even that involved.

We ran down the path with great strides. Wherever I was going, it was without a weapon, without even the use of my own feet, perhaps finally without the use of my other parts, even the use of my sense, and I felt if something were not done, and done soon, this would be the doom of us all.

We did not go to the gate, but instead my left boot took a step onto a fence rail, and I flung my right leg over the top. Next, my left leg was flung over, and then I saw the only chance I was going to have. I was hanging on to the fence and the boots were ready to jump to the ground and run up the roadway. But my arms were now in my own power. The boots jumped to the ground just as I wrapped both my arms around the top rail of the fence. I fell forward onto that rail and hugged it as tightly as its bark once had, and my feet turned and twisted as the boots tried to carry me off. I clutched at the fence, stretched out like a night crawler half out of his hole. The boots kicked and clomped, twisted, turned, and in mad, frantic frustration banged me this way and that against the fence, until I was bruised and crying from the pain, holding on for life and in despair that there would be no end to the contest until my arms were torn from my body and I was carried off a horrible broken and bleeding stump to greet my mother and father without even the arms to hug them before we were brought to our end.

Surely that *would* have been the end to the struggle, but there was something in it to my favor. In the violence of their kicking, one of the boots kicked the other boot off, and then, one of my feet being free and under my command, I kicked at the heel of the remaining boot and it dropped to the ground. Exhausted, I let go the fence and fell into the weeds, but I knew I hadn't but a few seconds and no time to rest, for the boots had stepped up onto the road and were dancing the enchanting circle, and soon they would call for my feet again. I rolled the few feet down the fence line to the gate. The vertical bars of the gate were spaced close together, and I wedged both my feet between two of the bars and turned onto my side, locking my feet into the gate like the turn of a key, holding them there with the whole weight of my body flattened on the gate path. Just then the boots completed the third circle and called out:

> "Inside my bones,
> Inside my meat,

Inside my heart,
Inside my FEET!"

It was two hours at least before sunrise, and longer before I could have any hope of someone passing on the road. I lay there in the gate path, clutching at the gravel until my hands were bleeding, trying to keep my feet tightly locked in the gate as they fought to wrench free and go to the boots, which danced on the roadway in the enslaving circles and many times called that terrible enchantment to my feet. Surely, I thought, my feet would be torn off by this strife and my life's blood spent at that place. But finally the sun rose, and because evil is haunted by the light, the boots ran off down the road and into the dark forest. I saw them go, and remembered no more.

Harley was licking my face and the sun was high when I woke up. My feet were still locked in the fence. I removed myself tenderly and limped back up to the house. My pajamas were torn to rags from writhing in the gravel, and it was all I could do to take care of the animals before I took care of myself. Settling in a tub of water up to my neck, a large kettle close at hand for refreshing the tub, I let the pain soak out and thought about the boots. They would be back, I was sure of it. They were jealous boots, and they had lost their prize. They would be back at midnight.

It was early afternoon yet, and I would have had time to ride to our nearest neighbor and bring grown-up help back with me. Three or four men might be found who would wait with me, grim and ready for the return of the boots. But I concluded that this was not the answer. The boots were enchanted, that much was sure, and enchantments have a wary sort of intelligence. I doubted that the boots would come if anyone but myself alone were in the house. Yes, they would return for me alone, and *only* if I were alone. I was not happy with this conclusion, but I was certain it was so. The coming night's work was up to me. I must allow the boots to come and attempt to take me away into the forest. But this time I was going to be ready for them.

After soaking for an hour in the tub, I doctored my feet with ointments and bandaged them in soft clean linen. I put on slippers then, for my feet were too swollen for my boots, and took the shotgun and Harley with me and limped up to the road. We found the place where the boots had entered the forest. We walked a little way in. Even in the daytime it was dark in there. The trees were set close together and the brush was high. You could not walk fifty feet without offering an ambush to anyone who waited in there. The track of the boots headed straight into the crowding darkness. Harley and I walked a few yards, but stopped while the roadway was yet in sight. I pointed the gun into the sky and shot off both barrels, and listened. The trees muffled even the echo, and there was no other sound from the inner forest. Perhaps my mother and father were already dead. No—but perhaps they were bound and gagged, or too far away to hear. Then let the shotgun blasts be an invitation to the boots, a challenge for them to come and get me this night. Let them come with their strange magic. I would be ready for them with some plain business to kill an enchantment.

Upon returning to the house, I tied Harley to a porch post. I went inside and rigged up a sort of modified rabbit snare with thin wire, cut a hunk of bacon from a side, and went out to the woodpile. I set the bacon and the loop of the snare at a rat's runway under the woodpile, took the other end of the wire and climbed up on top of the wood and lay quiet. Fifteen minutes later I noosed my first rat, a big bold one, and took him inside. I put him in our great iron pot that hung over the fire to cook the huge spicy stews when we had company. I lifted the pot down onto the floor. The rat ran around in the bottom. I left him to meditate on the particular infinity of pot bottoms and went outside to the woodpile again. It took half an hour to get the second rat, an even larger beast, who snapped and struggled in the noose and looked at me with a cunning and hateful glare. I think he was a general. Into the pot with him also, and then to other business.

I boiled two potatoes with cabbage and ate that with a hunk of salt beef. It was late afternoon by then. The show would not start until midnight. There was plenty of time yet, so I sat back in father's great stuffed chair to take a nap, and all the dim afternoon until twilight I slept. And I dreamed. I dreamed wild and eerie dreams that ran like knotted rope burning through the crystal hands that hold the sleeping brain, and I awoke with a greater fear of the coming night than I had carried to sleep with me. The sun had set. I got busy with my work.

First I fed Harley and cared for the other animals, then washed the dishes. Since I would be staying downstairs, I lit the fire and stood looking into it for a while, thinking my plan over to discover if there was any fault with it. The rats scurried around in the pot. Probably they were hungry. That was good. Barefoot, for my feet were still too swollen to get into boots, I pulled my chair to my defensive position in front of the door. Next to it I set a small table. Then I gathered my weapons to hand. I got a small sledgehammer and two spikes from the toolbox and set them on the table. Then I went to the pantry for a jar of honey and set it on the table also. It was dark out now. From the mantel, I took the nearly full box of shotgun shells and set them next to the honey. I went outside and tied Harley to a nearby tree. I didn't want him on the porch to interfere with the boots' arrival. While I was out there, shotgun in hand, I walked down to the fence and took a look up the roadway. Nothing in sight, and no sound. No, not yet. It was too early.

I returned to the house, bolted the door and attached my three pieces of twine as I had the night before, then sat down in my chair. I tested this little invention again, and it worked fine. With rod and rag and oil, I cleaned the shotgun and loaded both barrels. The fire was getting low and I set two large logs into it. Again I sat down, and waited. It was a little after nine o'clock. I was ready, and wide awake.

It was midnight when the boots had come before, and at midnight they would come again. Then I would bring them inside, the same as before. Then they would dance the enchanting dance and say the enchanting rhyme. And then . . . well, we would see what would happen then. I glanced at the table, at the sledgehammer and spikes, the jar of honey and the shotgun shells. Yes, we would see what would happen then. I rubbed the freshly oiled stock of the shotgun and listened to the rats running in the iron pot. The smaller one was trying to go over the top and kept falling on his back. The general was squealing orders at him. I waited.

The clock above the stove said 10:30 when next I looked. Was it working? Yes, it was ticking. I watched it sleepily. How slowly a clock's minute hand moves. The small brass circus inside the clock seemed weary now after wheeling and swinging and spinning and clicking all day. Quitting time. All the glittering performers that spin the bright rings had gone back to their trucks and trailers and tents, and now only the sluggish caretakers with their brooms and rakes ran the works, pushing slowly around the rings where all day there had been the lively prancing of brass horses with ruby eyes and the tumbling of spring-steel clowns. Would everyone fall dead before midnight, and time come to an end? I shook my head. Oh, oh. What nonsense was I thinking? I was on the edge of sleep. I went to the sink and dashed some water in my face. Eleven o'clock. I wound the clock.

I made a quick trip to the pantry and put some dried apricots on the table. I sat down again and chewed the dried apricots. Good, I was awake again. When the apricots were gone I took a couple of shells from the box and read the printing on the side of them. I kept my eyes away from the clock. Time would go faster that way. Leaning my head back, I looked up through the hole I had blasted in the roof the night before. The great star giant Orion would pass that way soon. I wondered about him, for I knew something of his story. When he lived on earth he was killed by a woman who loved him. But if she loved him, why did she kill him? It didn't make any sense to me. I guess it didn't make any sense to Orion, either, for that great hunter has been hunting among the stars for thousands of years, yet is so vexed and confused by what has happened to him that he is forever stumbling over a small star rabbit and never even notices. My mind wandered on to rabbit snares for a while, and I wondered about rabbit families and what they were like, and if they missed a father or mother rabbit who was snared. While I was pondering this disturbing possibility, the knock came at the door. It was the same scuffling toe-end-of-the-boot knock that I knew well now. I looked at the clock. It was exactly midnight.

Just in case, I cocked both hammers of the shotgun, then with my twine I slid the bolt and opened the door. There were the boots, and otherwise no sight or sound of any living soul, just as I had expected. I gently let down the hammers of the shotgun and walked to the door. Perfectly quiet outside. I could make out the shape of Harley sleeping by the tree. I took the tops of the boots in one hand, lifted them inside and set them just a short distance away from my fortress chair. After bolting the door again I sat down and studied the boots. The first part of this strange play was done, and in a short while the second act would begin. The boots would dance and call for my feet.

But as the boots sat there before me right then, they were perfectly harmless. I could have stepped into them and out again with no danger. The enchantment, however it was controlled, whatever the terms of its wickedness, abandoned the boots on the doorstep after knocking. Therefore, they appeared as ordinary boots, and although they were extraordinarily large, it was outside the range of a generous-hearted and honest man's intuition that there was anything wrong about them, for the evil had for the moment stepped out. Otherwise, I believe they would never have been brought into a house, certainly not a house where God-fearing folks dwelled. It was only after the boots had gained their entrance, and quiet had settled, that the enchantment would return to work its mischief. My plan was to catch that enchantment and destroy it, to trap it when it returned to the boots, and eliminate it entirely. And so, with the enchantment and its power destroyed, my prayer was that my mother and father would be able to return from the forest.

The evil thing that now waited would come to no door or window, and there was no lock so secure or wall so stout that could keep it away. It would come to the boots out of the very air, collecting itself together like a mist perhaps, as a dank vapor collects in a tomb. It made no sound and had no smell, so Harley knew nothing of it. Even now he slept peacefully. I waited. In a few minutes I began to feel a strange thin presence in the room, an airy and vaporous thing that came in with a chill. It was coming. I laid the shotgun aside and picked up the sledgehammer and the two spikes and waited on the edge of my chair.

Then, with the slightest sucking sound like the last swirl of water going down a drain, the boots came alive with the enchantment and took a step. I waited just a moment, until the second step of the enchanting circle was begun, then I leaped at the boots and in half a dozen blows with the sledgehammer I drove a spike through the toe of each boot, pounding them flat and tight to the floor. I had them! And now they would die! I reached for the jar of honey, unscrewed the lid, crammed my hand inside and smeared great globs of honey all over the boots, inside and out. Then I lugged the great iron pot nearer and with a hard effort lifted it up. As quickly as my strength could manage I tipped it upside down as I brought it banging down over the boots, completely covering them. The rats stayed inside. I put an ear to the pot. The rats were busy already. They were eating the sweet, honey-smeared boots!

And that's that, I thought, as I washed my hands and listened to the rats chewing up the boots. That would be the end of the boots and the enchantment. If my folks did not come back that night, next day I would go into the forest and find them. Even though I feared that, I would have no worry about enchanted boots taking the power of my feet or hands from me. I trusted the shotgun to take care of whatever else was in there. But I could not have used the shotgun to blow up the boots, you understand, because that would only have blasted them to shreds, into so many little enchantments perhaps, and still with power if they could somehow collect themselves together. No. The boots would have to be destroyed entirely, and to be digested in the bellies of two rats would do nicely for that. The only other plan which I had considered was to pour kerosene over them and burn them, but I cast off this plan for fear that I might also burn down the house.

The exercise in the pot had been good for the rats' appetites. They ate at the honey-smeared boots for two hours, and they did not stop chewing slowly, as if they were getting full, but stopped suddenly as if there were nothing else left under the pot to eat. I lifted an edge of the pot and rolled it aside. The boots were completely gone. Two spike-heads, shiny from the teeth of the gnawing rats, showed where they had been. But the rats themselves! They were huge! Of course I had expected them to be a great deal fatter from eating the boots, but they had grown entirely and all over, and each was now as long as the boots had been. And they rushed out at me!

I jumped back in alarm, looking for something to leap onto, but before I could get away both rats were at my feet. They weren't biting at me, thank God, for they could have taken my toes off with no trouble, but they began *snuggling* about my feet, *crowding* against my feet, each rat at a different foot, pushing their bristly bodies next to my feet as if they were great hairy slippers that wanted to be put on. Yes—I understood exactly! The enchantment had *not* been destroyed, but had merely entered the bodies of the rats, and they ran in circles around my feet and snuggled as if expecting that I could jump right inside their skins. They squealed all this while, and perhaps it was the enchanting rhyme they were saying, but it had no effect in rat language if it was.

Tripping and stumbling over them, I walked over to the pot. Carefully, ready to snatch back at the slightest show of savagery, I put a hand down to my feet. The rats ignored it. They were interested in my feet only. The enchantment, after all, was not meant to harm me, but only to take me away. I grabbed them both by their necks, lifted them and dumped them into the pot. I had to have some time to think this over. I sat down in my chair. Now what should I do?

Several things were important. For the moment I had the advantage over the enchantment, but that might not last. Dawn and a new day might release greater dangers on myself and the life of my folks, if they were yet alive. The answer I needed had to take advantage of the moment, the imprisonment of the enchantment, and the use of the rats.

The answer that I came up with I did not particularly like, but it seemed the only answer, and time was moving on. Things were going to be much more risky than I had ever figured. I was going to have to enter the forest that night and visit whatever was the master of this magic. But my mother and father were there, and I was going to have to do what I could, although I had barely enough courage to get busy with my next tasks.

Taking up my ball of twine again, I twisted and knotted, and tried out two or three styles until I invented what looked to be a couple of workable rat harnesses. It was fortunate that the rats were harmless, for I could not have managed otherwise. I reached into the pot and slipped both rats into harness, leading the reins over the side of the pot. Once more I checked the shotgun and leaned it against the table. I filled a lantern and fetched a hatchet. Then I put on my jacket and filled a pocket with shotgun shells. That was all I would need for the journey outside. I investigated the rats again. They had tangled the reins of the harness, for they were still running circles, but I soon had that straightened out. I rolled the pot aside and let them out.

They scurried to my feet. With reins held tightly I kept their heads up and forward and stepped onto their broad backs. Their rough hair gave footing to my bare feet, and after a few tries I managed to balance on them. This suited them fine. The enchantment supposed it had captured my feet, although I could step off at any time I chose. I gave the rats their head. They ran to the door and I stayed aboard. They put their noses to the crack, searching for a way to get out. Fine, it was exactly as I figured. The rats would carry me into the forest, and now I had some control. Jerking the reins, I managed to pull the rats from the door. I rode them around the room a few times, turning them this way and that and stopping them at will with a hard pull on the reins. They obeyed me with a grudge, but they did obey me, and in twenty minutes I could ride them as well as I could a goat, which is not easy, but it can be done. So I was ready.

I rode them over to the table and looped the lantern in the crook of my left arm, and in that hand I took up the shotgun. I stuck the hatchet in my belt, took the reins in my right hand and rode the rats to the front door. This was my last chance to give it all up. When I opened that door there would be no going back. I paused a moment. The rats squealed and paced back and forth at the edge of the door. Perhaps the enchantment had some little power left, for although I was very afraid, I was also excited, almost eager to go. And no matter what other danger, my mother and father were somewhere in that forest. All right then. I opened the door, and with shotgun, lantern, hatchet, and a pocket full of shells I rode out barefoot on the boot-fattened rats.

Harley began to bark, and I was glad he was tied up. He would have attacked the rats, putting a quick end to my plan. The rats headed for the fence and would have knocked me silly going underneath it, but I pulled them off their track and to the gate. They could have their own way after we got onto the road. As soon as we were through the gate and on the road I loosed the reins and off we went, the rats full of enchantment under their trembling load. We entered the forest at exactly the place where the boots had entered it on the previous night. The rats dashed into the dark brush. Switching the reins to the hand with the shotgun, I pulled the hatchet from my belt with my other hand. It was a crowded forest, and trees often came within reach. I swung at them with the hatchet as I passed, taking out hunks of bark or scallops off limbs, blazing a trail to find the way back, please God I should ever be coming back.

The brush jabbed and tore at me as we ran on into the darkness, and three times I was knocked off the rats. But I held tightly to the reins, wrapped twice around my fist, and with as much luck as skill I managed to hold the lantern upright. It could have broken and slopped me with kerosene, reducing me in a glory of fire to a small heroic handful of cinders with not even a boot nail left to tell the story. Once or twice I fell and was dragged for a few feet by the rats, who seemed nearly crazy with ambition to get wherever we were going and evidently hadn't noticed that I wasn't with them any longer. But I yanked them to a stop and took the opportunity to make some good blazes on nearby trees, for many of my headlong running swings had amounted to no more than thin cuts. Then I mounted my snake-tailed steeds and we were on our way again.

We were perhaps a mile into the forest when the limb of a tree knocked the shotgun out of my hand, and I could not stop the rats to retrieve it. We were nearer the source of the enchantment now, and the furious desire of the rats was growing stronger as we approached that burning center. So I only held on and continued blazing at the trees with the hatchet, concerned now that it should remain sharp at the end of our mad rushing journey, for with the loss of the shotgun it was the only weapon I had left.

How deeply into the woods did we go? I don't know, and no doubt in worry and pain and fear I might have said that the ride lasted for hours, but probably we went no farther into the forest than two miles or so, and I rode the maniac rats for no longer than about forty minutes. I had given up trying to watch ahead by the light of the lantern. I held it next to my chest to protect it from being torn from my grip, and the near and bright light of it made the distance even darker. I held my head cocked forward and to the side to save my eyes from being poked out by branches, and gripped the hatchet ready to take a hit at whatever close and solid shape we passed. Sometimes I hit a tree, sometimes not, the wasted effort nearly throwing me from the backs of the rats. If my mother and father had managed to escape and were walking out that way I would probably have taken both their heads off with a single stroke, mistaking them for trees.

Somewhere near the end of our journey my feet began to feel wet. Fearing I was cut badly and bleeding, I bent my knees to investigate. The rats were foaming at the mouth; they turned their red eyes upward to me, weary of the burden and hating it, and yet in their bowels the enchantment burned with the same ferocity and they must go on. They were nearly dead from exhaustion. I pulled them back as much as I could so they would not die on me.

We reached a stream. The sound of the running water was refreshing, and I wished I could go to the edge and wash my wounds, but the rats went directly to a log that stretched to the other side, and we went across. It was difficult footing, and the rats were unsteady. I was nearly pitched over the side but I grabbed a snag to save myself, and in doing so I lost the hatchet. It dropped into the darkness, splashing somewhere below in the stream. I could probably not have found it even in the daylight. Now I had no weapon at all. We gained the other side of the stream safely. The rats were coughing blood. Surely they were near death. They stumbled and lurched, at the end of their strength, the flame of the enchantment almost dead in them except for the bright sparks of their eyes. After leaving the log bridge, I crouched over, coaxing them on, my head close to the heat and fumes of the lantern.

Then, without the slightest notice so that I could prepare myself or give thought or devise a plan, the rats on their last breath crawled into a small clearing and stopped. I looked up. A great bonfire was roaring in the center of the clearing. Off to the side there was a cage made of saplings, in which stood both my mother and my father. My mother was in her nightgown, without her robe, and father was naked. Sitting near the fire on a great log was a barefoot giant. He looked at me with the delight of a spider who has brought a prize to the hot and hungry center of its web, and he roared, "HAH! I THOUGHT THERE WAS ANOTHER ONE!"

At that moment, both rats sniffed, coughed, and died. Feeling a slight sense of pity for them, I slipped from their backs as they rolled over. I dropped the reins and stood staring at the giant, and he at me.

My mother and father cried out to me through the bars of their cage. "Run, run! Save yourself!"

"DON'T SHOUT!" the giant roared at them. He was of awesome size, an old giant with a bald head, although around his ears there were fringes of white hair which hung to his shoulders, and he had a great drooping mustache. He was leaning forward with his forearms resting on his legs. In his right hand he held a needle as long as a bayonet, and in his left hand, smoothed across his knee, was his work. I recognized the material. It was my father's nightshirt and my mother's robe he was sewing at, sewing them to-gether. Then I saw that the giant's jacket was made up of a patchwork of coats, dresses, nightgowns, nightshirts and other such human-sized clothes. Bonfire shadows danced on his face. He smiled a sweet and snaggled smile at me, and said, only a little softer than when last he had spoken,

"IS THAT A WOOL JACKET YOU HAVE ON, BOY?"

He was looking at me past the side of the fire, so he couldn't see that I wasn't standing in his boots.

"Run!" my father shouted. "Run and save yourself!"

"STOP THAT SHOUTING!" the giant roared. He picked up a pair of scissors as long as a sword and snapped them at me. "THESE SCISSORS HAVE SHARP LEGS, BOY. DO YOU WANT THEM TO CHASE YOU?"

I believed that they could, and I had not come that far to run away. I spoke to the giant. "Why have you taken my folks' clothes? What are you going to do to them?"

"WHAT DID YOU SAY?" said the giant, cupping an ear toward me. I repeated my question. "I NEVER COOK ANYONE WITH THEIR CLOTHES ON. THAT'S FOOLISH. WOULD YOU COOK A RABBIT WITHOUT SKINNING IT?"

"Are you going to eat them?" I asked, now noticing forked sticks on each side of the fire, to cradle the spit for roasting meat. "Cook and *eat* them?" I croaked. But of course I knew the answer. The giant was wearing the evidence of his past meals, his coat made of the nightclothes of his victims. I was horrified.

"OF COURSE I'M GOING TO COOK THEM. HOW CAN I EAT THEM IF I DON'T COOK THEM? I DON'T EAT PEOPLE RAW. I'M NOT A MONSTER, YOU KNOW!"

"But why? What have they done? Why are you going to eat them?" This meant nothing to me, but I was stalling, looking about, trying to think of something to do, some plan, some weapon. . . .

"WHAT?" the giant roared.

259

I said, "What have they *done?*"

"HOW SHOULD I KNOW WHAT THEY'VE DONE? THEY KNOW WHAT THEY'VE DONE, I DON'T. BUT I EAT EVERYONE WHO CAN'T ANSWER THE QUESTION."

"The question?"

"I WOULD GO HUNGRY AND BE HAPPY IF ANYONE COULD ANSWER THE QUESTION."

"What question is that?" I asked. His needle. A weapon. If only I could get hold of his needle. But he held it tightly in his fingers, and now he took another stitch at his work and looked up.

"DO YOU WANT TO KNOW THE QUESTION?"

"Yes, if you please."

"WHAT?"

"YES," I yelled. "IF YOU PLEASE."

He looked to his work again. "It's not likely you'd know the answer. Your parents didn't know, either." The giant held his sewing up and shook it out, then smoothed it over his knee again. "Many long times I asked the question of myself, but I couldn't find the answer. I asked and asked and asked, but I got no answer. I decided to see if anyone else could answer the question, so I sent my boots out for them." He squinted at me over the fire. "DO YOU WANT TO KNOW WHAT THE QUESTION IS?"

"Yes, please." I was swinging the lantern from side to side, looking all about the ground near me. A sharp stick might do, even a small club.

"DO YOU WANT TO KNOW WHAT THE QUESTION IS?" repeated the giant.

"YES!" I yelled at him.

"IF YOU KNOW THE ANSWER, I WON'T EAT YOU. WHY ARE YOU SWINGING THAT LANTERN ABOUT?"

"I'm nervous," I said. "I hope you won't eat me."

"That's understandable," said the giant. "Did I ask you if that's a wool jacket? I need more wool for a blanket. It gets cold, and I'm alone."

"Yes," I said. "It is."

"Good," said the giant, taking up his work and examining a hem. Then he went to sewing as if he had forgotten I was there. I was going to have to move from the spot to find a weapon. There was nothing at hand.

"BUT WHAT IS THE QUESTION?" I yelled at him.

"WHAT?" said the giant. "DO YOU HAVE A QUESTION?"

"I was talking about *your* question. The question you ask before you eat me."

"DO YOU WANT TO KNOW WHAT THE QUESTION IS?" asked the giant.

"Please," I said.

"The question is this," said the giant, folding his work and pointing the needle at me. "What became of the child that I was?"

I looked up at him. The giant touched the corner of his eye with the edge of my mother's robe. Then he jammed his needle into the log and glared at me.

"I LOVED THAT CHILD! I NEVER LOVED ANYONE ELSE, BUT I LOVED THAT CHILD. He was gentle, and sweet, and good, and beautiful, and happy. And I don't know what became of him. Nothing has . . . been the same since. I remember how he laughed, and . . ." The giant sniffed and wiped his nose with the robe. "I LOVED HIM."

I looked at my folks. They made a gesture of helplessness. They had no more idea than I did of what became of that child. The giant was caught up in his woe and bewilderment. I watched him, and for a minute forgot my plans for escape in wonder at seeing such a great person cry. He put the palms of his hands to his eyes and smeared at his tears.

"I loved that child so. I loved him," he said softly. He wiggled his needle loose from the log and spoke in nearly a whisper while he stared closely at its point, as if he were looking at a world vastly faraway in time and place. "The animals came to that child, and he was gentle and kind to them. They ate from his hand, and the birds sat on his shoulders. How I loved him, and even the trees loved him, and all day long there was singing in the wind and water and leaves, and the forest kept him warm and safe, and . . . and . . ."

The giant's eyes were full of tears. After a few melancholy stitches, he turned the needle between his fingers and again dreamed silently of those days. He spoke again. "I remember his face in the water. His eyes. How beautiful. I loved him so . . . his hair, his hands, his mouth . . ."

A slight motion of my lantern brought him back from this dream and he gazed toward me. I could not help but feel sorry for him. His eyes were full of tears, and he gazed at me out of those dark pools with a deep and kindly sadness from faraway. It was as if he were looking through the past at the very child he had lost, and I felt pity for him and was certain for a moment that this sorrowful and weeping giant would *not* eat us. But then, even as he looked at me, his awareness of the time and place came back to him and I saw his present intentions return to his watery eyes like two water snakes coming to the surface.

"WHAT BECAME OF THAT CHILD?" he roared. Now it was an accusation, as if *I* were at fault for that lost child and deserved to be eaten if I didn't confess at once.

"Did . . . did the child eat people, too?"

"NOT ONE!" said the giant. "Didn't I say he was good and gentle and sweet? Not a bite! He was innocent. It's ME who eats people, and I'm going to eat you, too."

"That's a terrible thing to do," I said.

"IT'S NOTHING," said the giant. "What difference does it make? What difference does anything make if you can't answer the question? Who cares? NOW! WHAT BECAME OF THE CHILD THAT I WAS? CAN YOU ANSWER THE QUESTION? I'M HUNGRY."

I looked at my folks again. Father was pointing his finger toward the giant's scissors. They looked too heavy for me to lift. I stalled some more. "So you send the boots out to get people?"

"I taught them everything they know. That poem they say was going around in my head for a long time, and it seemed a good enchantment for boots. Now they go get people for me. Are your trousers wool, too?"

"So you enchanted the boots?" I said. There was a pointed stick lying not far away. It looked like a spit. Ugh! This is what he ran through people to cook them on, I guessed. I wondered if I could lift it.

"I taught them what they say. It's a poem. It rhymes, doesn't it?"

I remembered what the boots chanted after they danced:

> *Inside my bones,*
> *Inside my meat,*
> *Inside my heart,*
> *Inside my FEET.*

"Yes," I said. "The words 'meat' and 'feet' rhyme. It rhymes perfectly."

"DOES IT RHYME?" the giant roared.

"YES!" I yelled.

"I thought it did," said the giant, patting his work out while he mumbled. "It was just going around in my head like that, and I taught it to the boots. I could have taught them other things. When I was younger I used to write poetry, you know."

"I didn't know," I said.

"I remember my first poem," said the giant. "I cornered a deer and was going to crush his head with my club when I saw it was afraid, and then I saw a tear in its eye and all at once came the words to my brain: 'fear,' 'deer,' and 'tear.' And I stopped with my club up in the air. I don't know why, just because for a second everything seemed sort of to fit together, you know. Mainly things never seem to fit together. So I sat down and thought of other words to see if anything else fit together, and I wrote my first poem. Do you want to hear it?"

"Of course," I said. And I did. Since I could find no

weapon to beat this giant's head with, maybe I could get some advantage by understanding him.

The giant bunched his work in his lap, straightened his shoulders, and recited very like a schoolchild:

> *"I went out one day to club a deer,*
> *I found a fat one pretty near,*
> *Fat and cornered and full of fear.*
> *I raised my club and then a tear*
> *Dripped from his eye, and in my ear*
> *I heard some words and they are here."*

After reciting, the giant asked, as if he truly cared for my opinion, "Do you like it?"

"I do," I said, wondering if the giant would let us go if I wept, which I would find easy enough to do. It seemed he might have a soft heart. But immediately he let me know that wasn't the answer.

"You know what's funny," said the giant. "I ran into that same deer the next time I went out clubbing. You know, like there's a kind of magic or something in poetry. So I cornered him again, and I thanked him and told him the poem. He appeared to like it, too. Then I smashed him."

Calmly, the giant took up his sewing again. "I made other poems, too." And he recited again.

> *"Inside of me a bone man lives,*
> *His teeth are mine, and mine are his.*
> *His company is scary, rather,*
> *But we always eat together."*

265

The giant touched his lip with his needle and mused on this poem. "That's not just right, of course, but I couldn't get it any better. 'Rather' and 'together' don't rhyme perfectly, do they?"

"That's true," I said. "You might have rhymed 'together' with 'weather,' or 'feather,' maybe, but then the whole poem . . ."

"I thought of that," said the giant. "And there's 'heather,' too, and 'leather' . . ."

But then I stopped listening. I *had* it! I had my plan. I had the weapon I was looking for, and poetry had given it to me. Because of this last poem being about teeth, and eating, I remembered the other rhyme the boots had said. There was the little verse they said when they carried me to the door.

> *Open wide and you will see*
> *What shall become of you and me.*
> OPEN WIDE!

That was it! Just what I was looking for. "Open wide!" The boots' own words would save us. It was a dangerous plan I had in mind. I was going to have to stand right up in the giant's lap to work it.

The giant was still musing on possible rhymes for "together." "Tether, whether, plether, mether, bether . . ."

"I think I know the answer to the question!" I called to him.

"What question?" Then he remembered his question. "WHAT? NO, YOU DON'T. NO ONE KNOWS THE ANSWER."

"But maybe I do," I said. "I'll have to come over to you to say it. May I?"

"Just come. The boots won't hold you now."

So I pretended to be stepping out of the boots. I walked around the fire and over to the giant. I was no higher than his knee. He put a hand down and fingered the sleeve of my jacket.

"That's good wool," he observed.

"But maybe I know the answer," I said. "And this is what I think. I think maybe I know what became of that child—"

"I loved him," interrupted the giant, and I was afraid he was going to start weeping again.

"I think maybe he's *inside* you," I said.

"Huh?" grunted the giant. "How can that be?"

"Let me show you," I said. "Let me climb up on your knee."

The giant grabbed me by the back of the coat and lifted me like a kitten. He set me on his knee.

"If that child is inside you," I said, "then I can look down your throat and see if he's down there."

"HOW WOULD HE GET INSIDE ME?" the giant yelled in my face. "I NEVER ATE HIM."

"I don't know. Maybe it's a mystery. But bend down and I'll look."

"All right," said the giant, and he lowered his head a bit.

"Open wide!" I said, using his own enchanted words against him. And he opened his mouth wide.

I grabbed his mustache for a handhold and looked up his

hairy nostrils. On the walk around the fire I had loosened and flipped off the cap of the kerosene well of the lantern. If the giant had had more teeth the plan would not have worked. But there was just room, and I shoved the whole lantern sideways into the giant's mouth! He lurched backward. I held tight to his mustache, wrapped my legs around his neck and reached into my pocket. I grabbed a handful of shotgun shells and threw them in after the lantern. Then I fell clear of the giant as he tumbled backward off the log gagging on the half-swallowed lantern and shotgun shells, then he belched and a roar of fire bellowed out of his mouth. He choked out screams and clutched at his throat, stumbled to his feet and ran off into the darkness, his mustache afire and streaming sparks behind him. Roaring like an open furnace he ran through the trees.

"He's headed for the stream!" my father cried. "The scissors, quick!"

That was my idea exactly. I dragged them over to the cage and father took them from the inside and worked against the vines that tied the bars together. Two of the bars fell, and my folks were free. "This way," I said. "I blazed a trail."

"My nightshirt," said father, who was still naked.

"No time," mother said. I took off my jacket and father tied the arms around in back of him. It fell in front like an apron. Then I ran back around the fire. My folks were close behind. I found the dead rats, and headed into the forest at that spot. We had run only a few seconds when there came a great explosion behind us. The fire had gotten to the shotgun shells.

"He didn't make it," said father. "He exploded."

"It's about time," said mother.

We hunted the trees for my hatchet marks. Smaller ex-plosions came from behind us as we ran on. We crossed the stream, which must have curved around to where the giant had run off. It was still dark, and we found as many blazes by feel as by sight. Behind us, all was quiet. We moved very slowly so we would not get lost, and I told my folks how I had saved myself on the fence, and how the rats had eaten the boots and that I had trained them and ridden them into the forest.

"Good boy," father kept saying. "Good boy."

We groped at the trees in the dark for a long while. The sun was just coming up when we found our way past my last tree blaze and out of the forest. We mounted the road-way and headed toward the house. Harley began barking as we came in the gate. And then we were home.

Mother and father stayed up, but I went to bed. I lay there stunned with tiredness and could not sleep. I thought of what I had done to the giant, and I was bothered. My folks came in. Mother had some hot chocolate for me. Father sat down and put his hand on my shoulder.

"I'm sorry about the giant," I said. "I don't like what happened to him."

"You had to do it," said father. "It was a brave thing, and you know how he was."

"But he was so sad about that lost child. I felt sorry for him."

"You did right," said father. "That was a good plan."

"He liked poetry, too. The deer poem was nice."

"Remember what happened to the deer," father said.

"I don't feel good about it," I said, and took a sip from the cup. "I didn't know that giants cried." Father patted my shoulder and nodded.

"Giants cry," he said.

"He was so sad," I said.

"That's no excuse for eating people," father said. He touched my head and stood up.

Mother kissed me on my temple. "Just pretend it didn't happen, dear."

Ah, mother.

"Sleep well, dear," she said, and they went downstairs.

I looked out the window. The great star giant Orion had long ago stepped below the horizon, and for a weary while before I slept I lay looking out at the coming day, and wondered what was going to become of the child that I was.